CATCHING SIRENS

SELENE J. KYLE

Contents

CHAPTER ONE

Mermaid Lagoon

"He's the prince, Aggie!" Sophie gushed.

Sophie was telling Agatha all about the boy she just met, who turned out to be some sea prince. In all honesty Agatha didn't even hear his name.

"We're going to be married!" Sophie exclaimed.

Agatha's eyes grew wide. "He already asked you!"

"Oh, he doesn't know yet." She winked.

Agatha rolled her eyes.

How could Sophie be in love with someone see just met! Like love only lasted a glance.

"Come on. I told Kiko I'd meet her at Mermaid Lagoon." Agatha said, swimming out of the room

"You don't even care about my prince. do you?" Sophie said, hurrying to keep up with her friend. "I bet you don't even remember his name!"

"Oh! Sure I do, Sophie!" Agatha said. "It was... ah... it was... It was Denzo!"

Sophie groaned. "His name was Denzel!"

"Fine, Fine." Agatha gave in. "But I was closer than usual!"

Sophie giggled. "Good job, Aggie."

The two girls continued to the surface to meet Kiko at the lagoon.

==================

"Aggie!" Kiko exclaimed and pulled Agatha into a big bear hug. She turned to Sophie and smiled. "And you."

The two girls pulled themselves onto the rocks with the other mermaids.

Agatha found a point shell and started to comb her hair, like the rest of the pod.

"Did you guys hear? About the Prince of Camelot?"

Agatha's head whipped towards Beatrix. "What about him?"

Beatrix looked like she would explode with excitement. "Reena, Millie and I saw him at Pirate Cove!"

Agatha raised an eyebrow. "Why is there a human Prince in Neverland?"

"No idea!" Millicent said. "But he's totally gorgeous!"

Agatha rolled her eyes. "Because that's all that matters."

"I know!" Reena gushed. She clearly didn't pick up on the fact that Agatha was being sarcastic.

"What were you all doing in Pirate Cove?" Sophie asked.

"The dolphins told us they saw the prince there so we went." Millicent said.

"And seeing a prince is worth the risk being captured be pirates?" Agatha sniffed.

"We were careful!" Beatrix argued. "And yes, yes it is."

Kiko gasped. "Maybe he's looking for a maiden to court!"

"Oh! I hope he'll except Mermaidens!" Millicent giggled.

"Doubt it." Agatha mumbled.

Beatrix ignored her. "He'll surely pick the fairest of them all!" She was now examining her reflection in a hand mirror.

"I'm sure he will," Sophie challenged.

Agatha frowned. "Forgotten about Denzo, have we?"

"It's Denzel!" Sophie snapped.

The mermaids heard a twinkling behind them. They all turned to see Tinkerbell frantically signalling at them. None of them new what she was doing. None of them spoke fairy.

"Tink?" Agatha wheezed. "Calm down. What is it?"

She was still making frantic signals at them.

"Somethings wrong..." Kiko panicked.

"We should dive!" Agatha said.

"No she might be trying to tell us something!" Beatrix said.

"But what if the pirates are coming!" Agatha reasoned. She turned to tinkerbell. "Tink, is that what it is? Pirates?"

She shook her head vigorously.

They started to hear shouting from the entrance of the lagoon, where the lagoon meets the ocean.

They all turned to see one of Camelot's ship drawing into the lagoon, heading straight for them.

"The prince!" Sophie exclaimed.

"He'll help us!" Beatrix beamed.

Agatha swallowed. "I don't have a good feeling about this..."

"Don't be such a worry wart, Agatha!" Kiko smiled. "It's alright!"

Agatha turned to Tinkerbell. She was still frantically dancing around for their attention and twinkling like a like winged bell.

"Tink is telling us otherwise!" Agatha yelled.

All of the mermaids turned to the fairy. She lit up when she saw their eyes on her, and she started signaling for them to dive.

A canon shot came from the boat in their direction. It missed.

Agatha swivelled to her friends. "Dive!" She cried.

All of them obeyed.

The pod swam underneath the boat to avoid being seen. They used there tails to try and break the wood of the boat, to make it sink. Planks started to break, but it wasn't enough. As the girls continued to bat the boat with their tails, Agatha and Sophie both swam up the get a view of the crew.

"Why are they attacking us!" Sophie said as she and Agatha surfaced.

Agatha glared up at the crew, that were yet to notice them. "I have no idea."

The other mermaids started to bob up around them.

"This is insane!" Kiko cried. Maybe she was a little too loud, because the whole crew, turned to them.

"There they are!" Cried a red haired boy.

The crew through nets of the boat and it swept toward them. They all scattered, and luckily none of them were caught.

The mermaids all resurfaced at different places around the boat to through them off. Sophie was facing the wrong way when she came up, so she didn't see when the net swept straight towards her.

But Agatha did.

Fast as lightning she swam to push her friend out of the way. As she reached her thrust her hands out and pushed Sophie out of the way of the net.

Agatha sighed in relief.

Her relief came too soon.

The net was meters away, then the next thing she knew it was surrounding her and she was rising out of the water.

All of the mermaids jumped out of the lagoon and grabbed hold of the net that held a screaming Agatha.

They started to weigh it down, but the crew on board were too strong, the pod started to rise towards the deck, bodies dangling off the net.

"LET GO!" Agatha screamed.

"What? We can't they'll get you!" Sophie sobbed.

Agatha sniffled. "It's fine! Let go and you will be safe!"

"NO!" They all cried.

"I'm sorry." Agatha whispered. Then started swinging around in the net, causing all of the mermaids to fall to the water, as she rose to her own doom.

CHAPTER TWO

Hunting

Tedros and Arthur stood on the docks as the crew prepared the ship for their departure.

Arthur turned to his son. "You will make me proud won't you?"

"Yes, father." Tedros said confidently.

The kingdom of Camelot, was in dark days. The kingdom was broke. The people were broke.

Last night it had been brought to the kings attention that the scales of a mermaid are quite valuable, and gather quite the profit.

So, King Arthur new that this would be their salvation! He got a crew together, with his son as captain, and here they were, about to set off on their journey to Neverland.

"Maybe I'll even fetch you two mermaids." Tedros cooed.

Arthur thumped him on the back. "That's my boy."

"The boat is ready, captain," Tristan called from the boat.

Tedros gave his father a nod an then climbed on board.

================================

It didn't take long for the crew to arrive in Neveland. They came across few inconveniences on their way.

Their boat pulled into pirate cove. There were pirate ships afloat in the water.

Tedros order Chaddick, Who was steering the ship, to pull up next to one.

They set out a plank connecting them to the other ship and Tedros walked across.

The pirates were reading to shoot him until he dropped a bag on gold pieces.

Their captain called for them to stand down. He had dark black dreadlocks, black breeches and a white undershirt to his black coat.

"What is the meaning of this?" The captain called.

"My name is Prince Tedr--"

"I know who you are." Snarled the captain. "Why are you here?"

Tedros inhaled. "I'm looking for a mermaid. If you point me in the right direction, there's more were that came from." He nodded towards the bag of gold on the floor.

The pirate captain nodded. "Mermaid Lagoon." He said. "By foot it's straight through Crocodile Crack. By boat, it's eastward around the island."

"How will I know when I'm there?" Tedros said, wanting to make sure he knew where he was going.

"When you see the mermaids sing on rocks," one of the pirates barked.

Tedros gave his men a wave, and they showed the pirates more sacks of gold. "If we find one. We'll come back and give you the rest."

"How do I know you'll come!"

"Because I promise," Tedros vowed. "And a prince never breaks a promise."

With that he was gone.

"You heard the man!" Tedros yelled to his men. "Eastwards!"

~~~~~~~

In the trees on sure, a little fairy in a green dress watched there interaction.

There was no time for her to get Pan. But the mermaids couldn't understand anything she said! What would she do.

Tink watched the boat sail out of Pirate Cove. There was no time.

She whisked through Crocodile crack, at lightning speed, to warn the mermaids of what she had seen.

~~~~~~~~

Tedros and the crew sailed Eastward.

"Get the nets ready." Tedros called to Dot and Anadil.

"On it!" They called back and the two rushed to set it up.

Tedros was looking out at the water when he saw three mermaids swimming along blissfully. One had blonde hair, another had red hair and the last had brown hair and Arabian skin.

He watched the three mermaids swim away into the mouth of a cove.

Gotcha. He thought watching them swim of into their little Lagoon.

When the boat sailed into the lagoon all of the Mermaids were looking at a little fairy. Until they saw there boat.

They looked happy to see them. He smirked.

"Fire the canon!" He yelled.

"Aye Aye Captain!" Hester replied and set it off.

He heard one of the mermaids scream to dive and he lost sight of them under the water.

He tensed. Frantically looking around the water for them.

Suddenly he felt the boat being bashed from below.

"Their under us!" Tedros shouted.

The boat started to rock and everyone held on tight to not go flying off.

Tedros was gripping the railing when he felt something bite his backside. He yowled and turned to see a very angry little fairy.

He laughed and trapped it under an empty wine glass.

He was so caught up with the fairy that he hadn't even realised the bashing had stopped.

"This is insane!" A girls voice cried.

He whipped around to see the pod had surfaced.

"There they are!" Tristan yelled, making their presence known to the crew.

Dot and Anadil through the net to the water and the pod scattered. They weren't under water for long, but when they surface they were all scattered around the boat.

"Go for that one," he said pointing at a mermaid with blonde hair and emerald eyes. Dot and Anadil obeyed and the net swept towards the mermaid.

Just as it almost had her, another mermaid came out of nowhere and pushed her out of the way.

Just as Tedros thought he'd lost himself a mermaid Dot and Anadil thrust the net forward and it wrapped around the one that pushed the blonde away.

Dot and Anadil started pulling the net out of the water. When the net hung a metre above the water all of the mermaids leapt out of the water and grabbed hold of the net.

The net started to lower. Dot and Anadil where no match.

Tedros run to help pull and the whole crew followed. The whole pod started to rise out of the water, hanging onto their friend in the net.

Tedros smiles widely. He started to count how many of them there were. His father would have, not one, not two, but six--

In that moment the mermaid in the net started to swing and buck until the other mermaids fell off into the lagoon below.

Tedros groaned and let go of the rope.

Only one.

Only one unlucky little mermaid.

CHAPTER THREE

The Crew of the Igraine

Tedros looked down at the mermaid unconscious on his deck.

She looks so peaceful. So beautiful. He thought.

She had a aqua tail, purple shells on her chest, hair as black as night with sea shells woven into it.

"Get her outta the net and take her below deck," Tedros commanded.

Dot and Anadil nodded and cut her loose.

When she was free Tedros bent down and ran his hand along her slimy tail. He looked up at her pale, beautiful face, and suddenly he felt sorry for her.

In a flash her eyes shot open, she pulled a shell out of her hair and stabbed him in the thigh with it.

He groaned in pain. He no longer felt sorry for the creature. Dot and Anadil seized her arms and dragged her towards the door to below deck, as she flapped around like a fish on dry land.

As the door slammed behind them, he started to feel the bashing on the bottom of the boat start up again.

Tedros groaned. He grabbed his pistol from his belt and started shooting blindly into the water, to ward them off.

It worked. The bashing stopped and the boat continued to sail towards the mouth of the lagoon.

==========================

Their boat sailed into Pirate Cove, where the pirates were awaiting his return.

They put the plank between the two ships and this time, their captain came across.

"Well?" He said. "Did you find 'er."

Tedros nodded.

Tristan and Chaddick chucked another few bags of gold over the gap and onto the floor of his ship.

His men scurried to the bag to see if the money was legitimate.

It was.

The captain gave Tedros a nod. "Pleasure doin' business wit' ya." The captain limped back over to his ship and they withdrew the plank.

Tedros turned back to the crew. "Set a course for Camelot."

========================

Bodgen looked down at the mermaid lying motionless on the cell floor.

"Er- would you like something to eat?" He stammered.

She didn't turn.

"Would you like to play with our tarot cards?" Willam asked, shuffling the deck.

She turned towards them, holding herself up on her elbows. "Sure," she sighed.

"Finally! Someone actually wants to play with us!" Willam exclaimed.

She smiled a little bit. Just a little bit.

"Everyone else on this ship is super boring," Bodgen said.

That made her laugh.

"What's you're name?" Bodgen asked.

"Agatha."

"Hello, Agatha. I'm Bodgen and this it Willam."

She gave a little nodded.

Willam laid down her first card.

Pisces.

"Enemies." Willam said.

"I think I know who that would be." She glanced up at the door to the deck.

Bodgen laughed and lay down the next card.

The Lovers.

Agatha frowned down at the card and looked up at the boys shocked faces.

"What does that mean?" She snapped.

The boys shared a look and then pulled their cards back in and shuffled them up.

"I think that's enough for today." Willam said, rushed.

Agatha huffed and rolled back over on the floor.

"We can bring you water if you'd like." Willam offered.

She hesitated but nodded slightly.

The boys rushed off to get it.

"Did you see it?" Bodgen hissed.

"Yes!" Willam snapped. "How could I not!"

They glanced over at Tedros, to make sure he couldn't hear them.

"Do you think it's him?" Willam asked.

"It has to be him." Bodgen said. "He's her enemy. The card said, enemies to lovers."

========================

Dot trudged down the steps to the brig with a bowl of spaghetti in her hand. She had declined to make their prisoner something, after all she was the boat's chef.

She hesitated at the bottom of the steps before walking over to the mermaids cell.

"Um, I don't know what you like... so a jus' made yer some spaghetti."

The mermaid turned to face her. "Spaghetti?"

"Yeah, spaghetti!" She paused. "Have you not heard of it?"

She shook her heard.

Dot smiled. "You have no idea what you've been missing out on!" She slid the bowl through the bars to her.

She hesitantly picked it up. Dot then slid a bag of cheese through. The mermaid eyed the bag strangely.

"It's good," Dot cheered. "Trust me!"

The mermaid sprinkled the bag of cheese over her spaghetti.

"I'm Dot by the way," she said.

"Agatha."

Agatha swirled the spaghetti around her fork and ate.

Dot bit her lip and crossed her fingers, hoping to have got results.

Agatha's face broke into a smile. "This is delicious!"

"You really like it!"

Agatha nodded. "Best food I've ever eaten."

======================

Hort was leaning against the railing next to Tedros, watching Nicola reading in the crows nest of the boat.

God, she's gorgeous. He thought.

"What's up with you?" He heard Chaddick say and zoned back into reality.

At first Hort thought that he was talking to him, until Tedros replied.

"I'm not sure it's just..." Tedros trailed off.

Hort waited for him to say something.

"Jus' what, mate?" Chaddick probed.

"Do you think that she could escape?" Tedros said.

Buffoon. Hort thought.

"How should I know?" Chaddick said, unsurely. "I know nothin' about their mermaid magic!"

"Nicola might." Hort suggested.

Tedros raised an eyebrow.

"Ya know, 'cause she's really smart!" Hort said.

"Alright." Tedros sighed and then called her down to them.

She climbed down and he sidled up to her. "What do you know about mermaids?"

========================

Nicola was curled up in the crows nest reading a book, when Tedros called her down.

She fumble climbed down the rope ladder too him.

She had no idea why Arthur had chosen her as part of the crew, maybe he didn't like her ghosting around the castle, and wanted the get rid of her.

"What do you know about mermaids?" The prince asked her.

Her eyebrows shot up. "Mermaids?"

"Yes, mermaids," he snapped. "You read a lot don't you? What have you read about mermaids?"

Nicola swallowed. She was not prepared for his question.

"W-w-well the goddess Atargatis transformed herself into a fish, because she accidentally killed her human lover--"

"I'm not interested in a history lesson, Nicola." The prince butted in. "I want to know if she's dangerous."

Nicola tensed. This boy deserved a punch in the face. They shouldn't have stopped her when the mermaid attacked him.

"Mermaids on land aren't dangerous," Nicola said. "Their powers come from the sea."

Tedros nodded. "Right. Well, get back to work."

What work? She wanted to say, but it was no use. She just nodded.

She looked over at Willam and Bodgen, who were whispering very secretively to each other and shuffling around their tarot cards. They weren't being useful, so she walked over to them.

As she did, they both immediately stopped talking and stood up straight.

"What are you guys--"

"Nothing!" They both cut off at the same time.

They weren't just useless. They were idiots.

She sighed and climbed back up into the crows nest and continued to read her book.

=======================

Agatha was curled up in her cell staring at her empty bowl of spaghetti.

She couldn't stop thinking about home. About how much she missed her friends already. About how she was long gone. Long out of their reach...

Before she knew it she had tears trickling down her dry cheek.

She was so home sick and alone. And she knew it was only going to get worse.

And no one was coming to save her.

CHAPTER FOUR

Fish Out of Water

From what she could see the sun had set.

Agatha didn't have a view of the out side, but she could see that the light that was seeping through the cracks in the planks had disappeared.

She pressed her eyes to a crack. She could see the water out side and the last sliver of sunlight disappearing on the horizon.

Agatha looked around out side her cell and saw the keys to the cell hanging. If she stuck her arm through the bars, she could reach them.

But there was no point in it. The prince had put them so close to mock her. Because if she did reach them and open the locked door--

What then? It's not like she could get herself on deck or even out of the brig! She had a tail, and it was like an anchor that a sailor couldn't get off the ocean floor.

The only logical way out for here was to break the wood of the ship. But she knew she couldn't. When their whole pod had bashed at the boat, it had barely down anything. She was just one measly mermaid.

Agatha felt her arms start to become itchy.

Oh, no. She thought.

She knew exactly what this was. When a mermaid is out of the water for too long their skin and scales starts to dry out. It starts with an itch, then skin starts to peel...

And then it doesn't take long for you to be dead.

She didn't know how long it would be until they reached Camelot. But she did know that she was being taken there because the king wanted her scales. And if she showed up all wrinkled and dry skinned, he would surely send her away, she could swim home.

All she had to do was make sure that they didn't put her in water before they got there!

The door to the brig opened and Agatha flinched. She looked down at her skin, starting to peel and lose its glow.

She heard slow foot step descend the steps.

Then the prince appeared at the bars of her cell.

She backed against the wall in the slightest way. Clearly he noticed.

"Do you fear me?" He mocked.

"Am I not right to?" She snapped.

"You fear me? Wait til you meet my father."

Agatha gritted her teeth. "Oh, I can't."

He opened his mouth to say something, then he hesitated when he saw her flaking scales. "What happened to you?"

Agatha bit the inside of her cheek. She needed to be careful.

"There are side affects to keeping a fish out of water." She said.

"How do I fix it?" He snarled.

"You don't." Agatha shrugged.

"Would putting you back in water fix it?"

Agatha slumped back with a huff. So much for being careful.

Tedros left the brig. Agatha thought he didn't care that she was in pain and simply, left. But he came back with a T-shirt soaked in salt water and dropped it on the floor in front of her.

She just looked at it blankly, without moving a muscles.

"I'm trying to help," he said through gritted teeth.

Agatha met his eyes. "No you're not. You're only doing this because my scales aren't worth a thing like this."

He balled his fist. "Just put the damn thing on!"

Agatha protested by folding her arms.

Tedros pulled his pistol out of it's holster and pointed it at her head. "Put. It. On."

She still didn't move. She was looking at the gun, with no hints of emotion on her face. Tedros was unsure of what she was doing. Did she not know what a gun was? Maybe she was just crazy.

She slowly inched across the floor towers him and pressed her forehead to the gun.

Tedros was shocked. But he didn't let it show on his face. He wouldn't give her the satisfaction.

"You're playing a very dangerous game here." He threatened. "I could shoot you right here."

"Can't you see that I want you to?" She pleaded, her face now flooded with emotion.

Now he was shocked, and didn't care if she saw it. "W-what?"

A tear rolled down her cheek. "Getting shot in the head is a far better way to die than getting skinned alive."

Tedros hardened. "My father isn't that cruel. He would shoot you before skinning you."

Agatha shook her head. "When a mermaid dies, her scales harden and lose their sheen, making them less valuable. The scales that are worth anything come from a mermaid that had them taken, while she was living." Her voice cracked.

It was how her mother had died. Dirty pirates had taken her. Pirates. This was a prince. A prince of good, supposedly!

She looked down at her scales, flaking more and more by the second. "My scales like this would still be worth more than they will when I'm dead."

Tedros's mouth hung open. How could his father wish such a cruel fait on an innocent girl just for gold?

His gun found its holster. "I won't force you to do anything. I just hope you'll do it."

With that he left the brig, leaving Agatha alone in the cold, dark cell.

Agatha's skin and scales started to itch. So much that she couldn't take it anymore. She reached over and squeezed the wet cloth over her tail. Magically her scales started to glow bright purple, then it settled to her natural aqua.

Agatha slumped down on the wooden cell bars.

Her plan had failed. She needed a new one.

She'd heard stories of other mermaids being held captive before. And most of those stories ended with the mermaid dead or with the mermaid tricking her captor into falling in love with her so he'd let her free.

The perfect plan.

CHAPTER FIVE

Rallying

S ophie couldn't stop crying.

Her best friend was gone.

Her best friend had saved her! And from such a horrible fate.

As soon as Tedros fired those shots into the water, the pod new that they were out numbered. So naturally, they went to Pan.

It took a while for them to get the message to him, because Tinkerbell vanished. They looked all over the lagoon for the fairy, but no one had seen her since Agatha yelled for them to dive. Maybe she hid? They just hoped that she was alright.

All of the mermaids now sat on the rocks of the lagoon with Peter sitting cross legged on the highest point.

It was dark out. The Igraine was long gone. They had been here for so long trying to think up a plan to save their brave friend. But they had nothing.

"We could fly after them!" Kiko said, breaking the silence the group was in, deep in their own thoughts and plans.

"Mermaid don't fly, Kiko!" Beatrix spat.

"Pan does!" Kiko shot back.

"We could pay the king to send her back!" Reena said.

"With What money?" Millicent said.

Reena was silent. They had none.

Pan smiled mischievous. "The pirate's money."

All of the girls stared at him.

"Pan, That's way too risky!" Beatrix gasped. "We'd be in more danger than Agatha is right now!"

"But what's life without a little risk." He winked.

"Even if we did get money how would we send word to the king in time?" Kiko reasoned.

Pan considered this. He looked like he was about to say something, like he had an amazing idea, his mouth opened--

It closed just as easily and all the mermaids groaned. He always left them on the edge of their seats and letting them down like that. But know of all times!

Sophie groaned. "There has to be a way to save Aggie! It'll be all my fault if those monsters skin her!" She started to cry even more at the thoughts of her poor friend's fate.

She wiped up her tears. Crying wouldn't get her friend back.

She closed her eyes runny through as many possibilities to save her friend as she could think of, in her head.

All of them fail.

She thought hard.

And there it was. Like a lightbulb switching on in a darkroom.

"A rescue mission." She said, eyes flashing open.

Beatrix rolled her eyes. "The boat is too far away for us to reach now--"

"I didn't say we had to rescue her."

Their eyes widened. They all knew exactly who would save Agatha.

"Well, What are we waiting for." Pan smirked.

CHAPTER SIX

Death Tunes

Tedros couldn't see a thing.

He was standing on the front of the boat, but fog masked the air around them. He could barely see 3 metres in front of him.

"Is there land here?" Tedros called back to Tristan, who was examining their map.

"There shouldn't be." He replied.

"Maybe we made a wrong turn a while back, cause there shouldn't be anything remotely near here." Chaddick said.

They were sailing very slowly to make sure that they didn't hit any rocks.

Then nowhere they heard singing. The most beautiful singing he'd ever heard, coming from beyond the fog.

"What is that?" Tedros shouted.

"I have no idea." Tristan said, entranced by the beauty voice.

The singing grew louder and louder. It was all around. But the source was still unknown.

In front of the the fog parted, to reveal a women.

She was sitting on a rock, hugging her knees. She wore a white dress, the dress had spots of blood on it and she had cuts all over her arms. She was soaking wet and appeared to be crying.

"Hello?" Tedros called out to her.

She just kept singing and crying.

Her voice was so beautiful. She probably needed his help. She might have been in a ship wreck or something.

Then he heard another voice. Then another. Then another. Fog started to clear and revealed that they were surrounded by sharp rocks. Each rock had another singing women on it.

"H-hello?" He repeated, this time it was more at a stutter. "Are you--"

He was to focused on them to finish. They were gorgeous. Chaddick sailed the boat towards them.

Suddenly the kitchen door swung open and Nicola, Dot, Hester and Anadil rushed out.

"Sirens!" Nicola screamed. But Tedros, Tristan, Chaddick, Hort, Bodgen And Willam, didn't even flinch.

Tedros couldn't hear a thing that they were shouting. All he could hear was singing.

The girls were rushing around the boat trying to get their attention and who knows what else.

Tedros just focused on the beautiful tune, when another voices started to sing. A voice more beautiful than the rest. A voice coming from the brig.

He slowly turned and made his way across the ship's deck to the brig. When he entered he saw Agatha leaning against the bars and singing.

He inched closer and leaned down at the cell. Agatha sat up and cupped his face through the bars. He met her chocolate brown eyes and fell deep into her trance. Their lips inched closer and touched.

She tasted like vanilla cream--

He suddenly jolted and he was on the deck of the ship, still listening the the women singing. He spun towards the brig.

It was all an illusion. He never really went down there.

He snapped out of that thought and shifted to the women singing.

He looked at there long wet hair, bloodied clothes and beautiful faces.

Actually they were starting to look less beautiful by the second. But he ignored it.

"Are you alright?" He said. "Would you like to come aboard? We can help you get home."

"No!" Nicola shouted.

Tedros spun. "What? They're hurt!"

"They're sirens!" Hester shot back.

Tedros's eyes widened. He pulled his pistol out and started to shoot at them.

As he did their song turned into laughter.

Nicola jabbed his arm. "You can't kill them like that!"

"Then how do we kill them then?" Tedros said, forcing himself not to shoot again.

"Well, a siren can only be killed if the mortal she seeks to lure doesn't fall under her spell!" Nicola shouted over the loud singing.

Tedros turned to the other men who were all looking eagerly at the sirens.

"We have to get them to stop listening somehow!" Anadil screamed above the noise.

Hester clubbed Tristan in the head, making him fall to the ground, unconscious.

"That'll do it," Dot said.

"No it won't!" Nicola yelled. "They have to resist it! At least one of them does!"

Nicola turned to Tedros, who had already gone back to ogling at the women. She moved to Hort and tried to get his attention. "Hort!"

He was looking out at the sirens still.

Nicola cupped his face with her hands. "Hort?" She whispered.

Hort met her eyes. "Nicola?" He said, confusion in his voice.

The sirens started to shriek in pain. Their whole bodies started to change. The no longer looked like beautiful maiden. They had gills on their necks, webbed finger and toes, dreadlocked hair, fins on their elbows, and scales covering patches of skin as well as torn clothing. There voice's didn't sounded beautiful, they sounded like snakes hissing in pain.

One of them climbed onto the boat in desperation. Reaching out to the door of the brig, before it collapsed dead on the deck.

They looked out at the water and discovered that they were all dead.

Wow. Tedros thought.

"What the hell just happened?" Bodgen said.

"Those pretty women just... just..." Chaddick said

"Those weren't pretty women!" Hester shrieked. "We came out here and you were all ogling at those disgusting things!"

"Are we just leaving Tristan or..." Dot's voice said in the background. They all ignored her.

"What? How did you not see them--" Willam started.

"That's their trick!" Nicola butted in. "They are meant to lure sailors to their deaths. They sing and men see them as beautiful women. But there illusion doesn't work on us girls."

"Ah," Hester smirked. "Must be a superior gender thing."

The girls nodded and the boys rolled their eyes.

"But they didn't attack us for no reason." Nicola said.

Tedros raised an eye brow. "No?"

"No. They came for her." Nicola glanced back at the door to the brig, where they could hear a low humming.

CHAPTER SEVEN

High Hopes

Agatha was in her cell trying not to cry. She knew that her plan would probably fail and she'd end up skinned. She knew that if Sophie were here she'd tell her to look on the bright side, to see that after the storm there'd be a rainbow.

But there was no bright side.

The rainbow wasn't that beautiful.

She pressed her eyes to a crack in the wall, that showed a view of the deck. There was fog surrounding the boat. The farthest she could see was Tedros standing at the front of the boat. A red haired boy was studying a map, another was steering the ship, one was doing something with a rope (she had no idea what) and Willam and Bodgen were sitting on upside down buckets dealing tarot cards.

The red-head and the one steering we're having a conversation with Tedros, but Agatha couldn't make out the words. She assumed the were discussing the fog.

Out of nowhere, she heard a voice. A beautiful voice.

Her eyes shot wide.

Sirens.

When sirens sing, to the mortal ear it just sounds like wordless beauty. But to mermaid it was different. They understood the language.

It was to hard to make out what she was saying, she was too far away. She just hoped that they were talking to her.

"What is that?" Tedros shouted. The crew had no idea what they were dealing with.

Agatha saw the fog part and it revealed a scaly siren.

At least, that's how she looked to Agatha. To the crew they probably saw some gorgeous and attractive women, that looked like she needed their help.

"Hello?" Tedros called out.

Now Agatha could hear what the siren was saying.

Agatha. The siren was repeating her name in different rhythms of song.

Her face broke into a smile.

She thumped her tail on the wall that the ocean sat on the other side of, to get the other sirens attention.

She heard another voice enter the chorus. Your friends have been worried. She said.

Tears came to her eyes, thinking about them.

Another voice joined. We'll save you.

Agatha was now sobbing, it was unclear of her emotion. She pressed her eyes to the crack again. All of the men were entranced.

"Hello?" Tedros repeated. "Are you--" he cut himself off.

It was going to work! She was going to be free--

She heard a door slam open and four women ran into view.

Agatha's stomach dropped. She didn't know there were so many women on board, she'd only seen Dot and an albino girl. Women could resist the sirens lures, and could snap the men out of the trance. She just hoped they didn't know that.

"Sirens!" A girl with dark skin screamed.

The men didn't so much as flinch. Agatha dug her nails into her palm and bit her lip.

The girl dashed around the boat yelling at each other and trying to get the boys attention.

She saw Tedros jolt and spin to where the door to the brig would be, but was out of her view. He turned back to the sirens. He didn't seem so out of it anymore.

"Are you alright?" He said. "Would you like to come aboard? We can help you get home."

"No!" Screamed the dark skinned girl.

Tedros spun. "What? They're hurt!"

"They're sirens!" A girl with red-streaked hair shot back.

Tedros's eyes widened. He pulled his pistol out and started to shoot at them.

As he did their song turned into laughter.

The dark skinned girl jabbed his arm. She said something but Agatha couldn't make it out. The conversation went back and fourth between Tedros and the girls, until the one with the red streaks clubbed one of the other men in the head, knocking him unconscious.

Um... Agatha thought. That was unnecessary.

"That'll do it," Dot said.

"No it won't!" yelled another girl. "They have to resist it! At least one of them does!"

Agatha gulped. They knew how to kill the sirens.

The same girl turned to Tedros, who had already gone back to ogling at the women. She moved to another and tried to get his attention. "Hort!"

He was looking out at the sirens still.

She cupped his face with her hands. "Hort?" She whispered.

The supposed 'Hort' met her eyes. "Nicola?" He said, confusion in his voice.

The sirens started to shriek in pain.

One of them climbed onto the boat in desperation. Reaching out to the door of the brig, before it collapsed dead on the deck.

Agatha looked out at the water and discovered that they were all dead.

She felt her heart in her throat.

"No." She choked. Tears spilled down her face. "No!"

She fell to the ground and sobbed harder. This time the emotion was unmistakably, pain. She sniffle and gasped for air.

She tried to take deep breaths. To wipe up her salty tears and stay strong. Keep the thought of seeing Sophie again brighten up her sorrow.

But she couldn't.

"But, they didn't attack us for no reason." A women's voice said.

"No?" Said Tedros's.

"No. They came for her." Agatha didn't have to see them to know the women was talking about her.

No. The rainbow wasn't beautiful.

It was ugly.

CHAPTER EIGHT

Shoulder To Cry On

When Tedros went down to the brig, Agatha was sobbing so hard that he began to worry she couldn't breath.

He tried to not feel like a monster as he spoke. "Did you summon them?" His voice was very stern, he did sound like a monster.

She wiped her nose. "No." Her voice was choked by tears.

This time when Tedros spoke, his voice was light and soft. "Then how did they know you were here?"

Agatha turned her body towards him ever so slightly. "The sea sends whispers."

What was he supposed to do with that? Tell the sea to shut up or else?

"What is that supposed to mean?" He said it a tad more aggressive and demanding.

"You wouldn't understand." Agatha said rolling over.

Tedros gripped the cell bars hard and you could see the blood draining, leaving his knuckles white.

He was going to scream at her to make sure they wouldn't be back. He was going to. Instead his fists unclenched, his intense glare faded, and his muscles loosened.

He knelt down on the ground and whispered.

"I'm sorry."

She scowled. "Yeah right." She was obviously being sarcastic.

"I'm only doing this for my father." He said.

Her ears perked up the slightest bit.

"Our kingdom is broke and--"

She whipped her head around. "Camelot? Broke?" She looked at him angrily. "Not broke. Just not rich enough!"

He was about to jump in but she spoke to quickly.

"All Neverland's money goes to Camelot! What did you do with it all? We've already given you enough! Now you take me! When I give up half of my gold when your goons come to collect!"

Tedros froze. He had no idea what she was talking about. His father sent people to take money from mermaids?

"W-What?" He stammered.

Her anger expression faded. "You don't know?"

"Kn-know what?" He demanded.

She itched her arm and skin came off. He noticed her skin and scales were all starting to flake. His eyes drifted to the dried out shirt in the corner of her cell.

She looked up at him. "Could you get me some wa--"

"No!" He cut off.

She flinched at the volume of his voice, which he instantly regretted raising.

He tried to calm himself, but his body was tense. "First, you will answer my question."

Tedros heard bells jingle behind him, but when he turned, there was no one there. He turned back to Agatha. "Did you here hear that!"

Agatha was now sitting upright and tensely straight. "Ah, n-no what are talking about?" She said it like she was lying, but why would she lie about not hearing bells?

He shrugged it off. "What do you know that I don't?"

She swallowed. "Once a month the king sends men to take money from the people of Neverland."

Tedros frowned. "Why?"

"He takes from us because we don't have a formal 'ruler.' Of course their's the chief, but he doesn't control, the mermaids, or the fairies, or the pirates, and most certainly not the lost boys."

"So why would you give your money to us?" Tedros asked.

Agatha shrugged. "We've heard stories of how brutal your men can be. We don't want to be on the other end of that."

"Does he do it to other kingdoms?"

"I wouldn't know. There aren't a lot of Ever kingdoms without rulers these days though." As she spoke her eyes kept drifting to something behind him, but the went back to him every time.

Tedros shut his eyes. "I can't believe I had no idea."

"Does your father keep a lot from you?" Agatha asked.

The question hit him hard. He always thought his father shared everything with him, but now he didn't know.

He stayed quiet.

"I'm sorry." Agatha whispered, pulling herself to him with the cell bars. They were now face to face. He found himself wondering if she really tasted like vanilla.

"No. Don't say that." He whispered back. "You're not the one who locked me in their brig."

The slightest smiled played on Agatha's lips. "You're just trying to make your father proud." She looked down, her face filled with sorrow. "I understand that."

"You do?" He asked.

She slowly looked up. "My father never wanted a daughter. He wanted a boy tha at would remind him of himself. Instead, he got me and my sister." Her voice broke. "He's never been proud of me." She whipped up her tears and sniffled. "Maybe he is now, that I saved Sophie. Or maybe he hasn't even realised I'm gone!" Agatha broke into more sobs. "All my life he's told me that I'm nothing if I don't marry well-- now I won't even have that chance!"

Tedros wanted to hold her and let her cry on his shoulder. But the bars were in his way. He grabbed the key off the hook and unlocked the cell. He slowly opened the door and entered. Agatha was sitting up in a ball, with he face in her tail (somewhere that would be her knees). Tedros put his arms around her and moved her head to his shoulder.

Tedros felt her tears stain his shirt, but he didn't care. It felt so right having her in his arms, he didn't want to let go. He'd let her ruin his shirt.

He held her for so long that he didn't realise that she'd stopped crying, and was just embracing him.

=========

Dot balanced trays of baked vegetables on her arms and head. The second she stepped out of the kitchen the crew swooped in and took a tray each.

She still had two plates; one for Tedros and one for the mermaid. She walked down to the brig to give them their trays. She wondered what Tedros was still doing down there and if her entering would through off his interrogation on the sirens. But she thought he would appreciate some food and went down.

When she got there Tedros was in the cell--

Her eyes widened. The were... hugging. Why? What had happened?

She snuck out of the brig and onto the deck. She walked right over to Hester, Anadil and Nicola.

"You won't believe what I just saw."

=======

Tedros and Agatha both jolted up when the heard the door to the brig slam shut.

Tedros looked up the stairs, when he saw no one there he turned back to Agatha. "I'm really sorry about your father."

She nodded. "I'm sorry about yours--"

The door to the brig was aggressively swung open and some one stomped down the stairs. Tedros and Agatha untangled the limbs and shot to opposite end of the cell.

Hester stoped at the bars. "What are you doing!" She demanded from Tedros.

Agatha recoiled against the wall, afraid. Tedros looked up at Hester. "Having a chat with our prisoner."

"It looked like you were doing more than having a 'chat' with her!" Hester yelled.

"Oh, really?" Tedros said, standing up. "What did it look like?"

She snarled at Agatha. "Looked like you two was in here neckin'!"

"Neckin'?" Agatha asked, unsure. Tedros glanced in her direction, clearly they didn't use such slang at Mermaid Lagoon.

Hester rolled her eyes. "Means kissing, Flipper!"

Agatha scowled at her new nickname.

Tedros balled his fist, his posture was tense and he spoke with irritation in his voice. "That's not what was going on."

"Might as well have been!" Hester growled. "She's your prisoner to your girlfriend!"

Tedros stepped close to Hester, so he was towering over her. "I think you've forgotten how to address your superior."

Hester took a breath and stood back. She was tense and flexing her jaw. "Forgive me your highness."

There was a long silence.

"All is forgiven." He said, as if without a care in the world. "Don't let it happen again."

Hester nodded. "Yes, captain."

Hester left leaving Tedros and Agatha in an uncomfortable silence.

When it was clear that there was nothing to be said Tedros started to leave--

Agatha grabbed his hand from her spot on the ground, and he slowly turned to her. When he looked into her eyes they we're silent pleading for him to stay-- but then she blinked and it was gone.

"Uh, w-water?" She said, it came out like a question.

Tedros jolted. "Of course!" He hadn't even thought of that, she'd probably been dry and in pain for their whole interaction. "Right away!"

He fumbled up the steps to fetch her the water. As he closed the door there was the most unmistakable sound of bells from down in the brig, but he shrugged it.What was the harm in having bells down there?

But little did he know they weren't bells and all.

They were the sound of a little flying stowaway.

CHAPTER NINE

The Stowaway

Tinkerbell had been trapped under that glass for the longest time. If the sirens hadn't come she never would have gotten out. The ship had become very rocky when those girls came out, so the glass fell, and Tinkerbell escape. Everyone was preoccupied so they didn't see her fly and hide in the crows nest.

She hid in there watching the whole thing, cheering the sirens on...

And being incredibly disappointed when the lost.

When Tedros opened the door to the brig, Tink slipped through behind him.

When they got there Agatha was in tears.

"Did you summon them?"Asked the prince. What an insensitive jerk. Tinkerbell thought. He doesn't even care that she's crying!

She wiped her nose. "No." Her voice was choked by tears.

This time when Tedros spoke, his voice was light and soft. "Then how did they know you were here?"

Agatha turned her body towards him ever so slightly. "The sea sends whispers."

Tinkerbell could see his frustration with this answer. "What is that supposed to mean?"

"You wouldn't understand." Agatha said rolling over.

Tedros gripped the cell bars hard and you could see the blood draining, leaving his knuckles white. Seeing him like this made Tink more scared than she already was. She was worried that he might hurt her--

He didn't. Instead his fists unclenched, his intense glare faded, and his muscles loosened.

He knelt down on the ground and whispered.

"I'm sorry."

She scowled. "Yeah right." She was obviously being sarcastic.

"I'm only doing this for my father." He said.

Her ears perked up the slightest bit. Tinkerbell felt herself go red with anger. What truck was he trying to play?

"Our kingdom is broke and--"

She whipped her head around. "Camelot? Broke?" She looked at him angrily. "Not broke. Just not rich enough!"

He was about to jump in but she spoke to quickly.

"All Neverland's money goes to Camelot! What did you do with it all? We've already given you enough! Now you take me! When I give up half of my gold when your goons come to collect!"

Tinkerbell welled with more anger at the thought.

"W-What?" Tedros stammered.

Her anger expression faded. "You don't know?"

"Kn-know what?" He demanded.

She itched her arm and skin came off. Tink noticed her skin and scales were all starting to flake. Tinkerbell's angry turned to worry. Had she not been given water to keep from drying up?

She looked up at him. "Could you get me some wa--"

"No!" He cut off.

Tinkerbell and Agatha both flinched at his volume. What a monster! Tinkerbell thought. She was in pain and he didn't care!

"First, you will answer my question."

Tinkerbell was so angry that she let out a jingle.

Tedros spun to her, but she ducked behind a barrel. She was quick enough to keep out of view of Tedros, but Agatha saw a glimpse of her.

"Did you here hear that!" The prince demanded.

"Ah, n-no what are talking about?" She said. Her voice made her sound like she was lieing but the prince shrugged it off.

Tedros went straight back to the point. "What do you know that I don't?"

She swallowed. "Once a month the king sends men to take money from the people of Neverland."

Tedros frowned. "Why?"

"He takes from us because we don't have a formal 'ruler.' Of course their's the chief, but he doesn't control, the mermaids, or the fairies, or the pirates, and most certainly not the lost boys."

"So why would you give your money to us?" Tedros asked. Tinkerbell peeked out from behind the barrel

Agatha shrugged. "We've heard stories of how brutal your men can be. We don't want to be on the other end of that."

"Does he do it to other kingdoms?"

"I wouldn't know. There aren't a lot of Ever kingdoms without rulers these days though." As she spoke her eyes kept drifting to Tinkerbell, but they went back to him every time.

Tedros shut his eyes. "I can't believe I had no idea."

"Does your father keep a lot from you?" Agatha asked.

He stayed quiet.

"I'm sorry." Agatha whispered, pulling herself to him with the cell bars. They were now face to face. Tinker wasn't sure where Agatha was going with this...

"No. Don't say that." He whispered back. "You're not the one who locked me in their brig."

The slightest smiled played on Agatha's lips. "You're just trying to make your father proud." She looked down, her face filled with sorrow. "I understand that."

"You do?" He asked.

She slowly looked up. "My father never wanted a daughter. He wanted a boy that would remind him of himself. Instead, he got me and my sister." Her voice broke. "He's never been proud of me." She whipped up her tears and sniffled. "Maybe he is now, that I saved Sophie. Or maybe he hasn't even realised I'm gone!" Agatha broke into more sobs. "All my life he's told me that I'm nothing if I don't marry well-- now I won't even have that chance!"

Tinkerbell wanted to comfort poor Agatha, but Tedros beat her to it.

He grabbed the key off the hook and unlocked the cell. He slowly opened the door and entered. Agatha was sitting up in a ball, with he face in her tail (somewhere that would be her knees). Tedros put his arms around her and moved her head to his shoulder.

Tinkerbell stayed in stunned silence, unsure of what to do. She couldn't believe Agatha was letting him hug her!

He held her for so long that Tinkerbell had stopped watching and was passing time by counting how many planks the brig was made of--

She saw the door open and a chubby women entered, holding two plates of vegetables. Tedros and Agatha didn't see her come in.

She suddenly stopped descending the steps when she saw the prince and mermaid hugging. She looked shocked and confused. The quickly left back up the steps slamming the door behind her.

Tedros and Agatha both jolted up when the heard the door slam shut.

Tedros looked up the stairs, when he saw no one there he turned back to Agatha. "I'm really sorry about your father."

She nodded. "I'm sorry about yours--"

The door to the brig was aggressively swung open and a women with red-streaked hair stomped down the stairs. Tedros and Agatha untangled their limbs and shot to opposite ends of the cell.

Hester stoped at the bars. "What are you doing!" She demanded from Tedros.

Agatha recoiled against the wall, afraid. Tedros looked up at Hester. "Having a chat with our prisoner."

"It looked like you were doing more than having a 'chat' with her!" Hester yelled.

"Oh, really?" Tedros said, standing up. "What did it look like?"

She snarled at Agatha. "Looked like you two was in here neckin'!"

"Neckin'?" Agatha asked, unsure. Tedros glanced in her direction. Tinkerbell had no idea what they were talking about--

Hester rolled her eyes. "Means kissing, Flipper!"

Agatha scowled at her new nickname.

Tedros balled his fist, his posture was tense and he spoke with irritation in his voice. "That's not what was going on."

"Might as well have been!" Hester growled. "She's your prisoner not your girlfriend!"

Tedros stepped close to Hester, so he was towering over her. "I think you've forgotten how to address your superior."

Tinkerbell held her breath.

Hester took a breath and stood back. She was tense and flexing her jaw. "Forgive me your highness."

There was a long silence.

"All is forgiven." He said, as if without a care in the world. "Don't let it happen again."

Hester nodded. "Yes, captain."

Hester left.

After a moment Tedros started to leave--

Agatha grabbed his hand from her spot on the ground, and he slowly turned to her. Tinkerbell's eyes widened, it looked as if she were pleading for him to stay-- but then she blinked and that look vanished.

"Uh, w-water?" She said, it came out like a question.

Tedros jolted. "Of course! Right away!"

He fumbled up the steps to fetch her the water.

When Tinkerbell was sure he couldn't here then she scurried through the air into Agatha's arms, letting out another jingle.

"Oh, Tink!" Agatha cried. "I had no idea you were here! I thought I was all alone."

Tink jingled a reply. Agatha stared. "I still can't understand you."

Tink nodded and looked down, sad. She wanted to asked Agatha what she was doing hugging that monster, but she couldn't.

"Do you have any ideas how to get outta here?" Agatha asked, hopeful.

Tink shook her head. Agatha sighed. "I've tried making him feel sorry for me... it's not really enough."

Ohhhh. Tinkerbell thought. That's what it was.

Agatha smirked. "Did you think that I would have done any of that if it wouldn't help get me out?"

Tink smiled guiltily and Agatha laughed.

======

Agatha lied.

At first she was doing it to get out... then she realised how easy he was to talk to, the whole thing about her dad just fell out. And as he held her it felt so right. She felt so safe in his arms, safer than she'd ever been.

It was strange. She never would've thought--

The door to the brig opened and Dot trudged done. She was carrying a bucket of water and a plate of food.

Tinkerbell quickly flew out of the cell and ducked behind the barrel.

Dot unlocked the cell and came in. She put the bucket and the plate down in front of her.

Dot twiddled her thumbs and whistled, as if she wanted to tell her something but didn't know how.

"Dot?" Agatha said.

Dot flinched. "Yes!"

"You alright?" Agatha raised an eyebrow.

Dot tried to hold it in, but couldn't help it. "WhenTedrossawthatyourvegetableswereall soggyheswapyourplatewithhis,becausehehadthebestcookedplateandhetoldmenottotellyou!"

Agatha's eyes widened. "Why did he do that?"

Dot went back to twiddling her thumbs. "I guess it means he care about you, and what's you to have the best."

Agatha scowled. "The best being I get skinned alive? Tell him how grateful I am!" She turned away from Dot.

"Okay... I will--"

"Don't you dare!" Agatha cut in. Dot clearly didn't know sarcasm.

"Um... well this is awkward." Dot said.

Thanks for stating the obvious.

"Um, can I..." Dot said in an uncomfortable high pitched voice.

"Yes, you can leave, Dot." Agatha said. Dot practically bolted out of the brig, making sure to lock Agatha's cell.

Tink flew back to her.

Agatha dunked the shirt in the bucket of water and ran it across her arms and the rest of her body, her skin stopped flaking and got back to its natural glow.

She glanced over at the food. It looked delicious. Tedros had traded his plate for hers which meant Tedros was up there eating soggy vegetables. She thought it was sweet that he did that for her but under the circumstances--

"You told her what?!" Tedros's voice roared from upstairs.

Tinkerbell and Agatha shared a worried look.

Poor Dot. Poor, poor Dot.

====

CHAPTER TEN

Missing You

The moment Tedros stepped out of the brig, everyone stared at him.

They clearly heard about him spooning with his prisoner.

He swallowed hard. "What are you all gawkin' at? Get back to work!" They all flinched and went back to what the were doing.

He went off to his cabin and sat at his desk. No matter how hard he tried to get her off his mind his thoughts kept drifting back Agatha.

The door swung open and Dot came in with dinner

Dot slid a tray of food in font of him. He heard his stomach grumble as he picked it up. When he glanced over at Dot, she held a plate with shrivelled up and soggy vegetables.

"Is that one for Agatha?" He asked.

"Yes... Why?" Dot replied.

"Um... I think I'll have that one instead." He swallowed.

Dot stared. "Why."

Tedros hesitated before swapping the two trays. "Just give that plate to her-- and don't tell her I had you swap them."

"A-alright?" Her nervous voice made her statement sound like a question.

Dot left, leaving him in his lonely cabin... still thinking about the mermaid in his brig.

He missed the weight of her head on his shoulder. It was strange. He'd never felt like this before... he didn't know what it was. Or what it meant.

It scared him.

He heard a shy knock on the door. When he opened it, it was Dot. Dot nervously smiled.

"What?" He said, know she'd done something.

"Well..." she held it in as long as possible. "IsortakindatoldAgathathatyouswitchedtheplatesbecauseyoudidn'twhatherhavingsoggyvegetables!"

Dot'd hoped that speeding up her voice would stop him from hearing her words, but he heard

"YOU TOLD HER WHAT!" He roared.

Dot winced. "I said--"

"I know what you said, Dot." Tedros said, falling onto his sofa and putting his head in his hands.

Dot stood awkwardly in the doorway, pretending to examining her boots, in hopes to make this less awkward.

"Please, leave me be, Dot." He moaned.

"Yes, captain." She said, and scurried off.

Agatha probably thought he was insane, now! She probably thought he was a sap! The worst part about this was he didn't know how he felt about her. If he did like her then why was he taking her to his father? Why wasn't he freeing her--

The door to his cabin opened. It was Chaddick.

"We have arrived."

=====

The moment that their ship docked, Arthur's men came up and barged into the brig. A few moments later, they came out with a sack moving and kicking at them.

Agatha. He could hear her crying. Tedros's heart ached seeing her like this.

He swallowed hard, if it hurt to see her like this, then he didn't want to know the pain of seeing her skinned.

=====

I'm sorry it was so short. :/I would have put it in the next chapter, it's just the next one is long, and all Sophie's and Pan's POV.

~Jen

CHAPTER ELEVEN

How to Rob a Pirate

Sophie furiously swan up towards Mermaid Lagoon.

She couldn't believe the incompetence of those sirens! You ask them to do one thing and they get themselves killed!

It goes to show:

You want something done right you do it yourself.

When she surfaced everyone was already there. She shooed Kiko if her rock and sat on it herself (it was her favourite.)

"So I believe it's time for my plan B..." Peter pushed.

"You mean take the pirates money? How on earth will we do that?" Beatrix sniped.

Peter leaned back on his rock. "How we do everything!"

Kiko raised an eyebrow. "Carelessly?"

Peter smirked. "Something like that."

=======

Peter perched on a tree spying on the pirates from afar. From where he stood he could see the mermaids hiding behind rocks at the tip of the cove, peeping on the pirates.

They were all a bit unsure of his plans, but Peter was so confident that they trusted him, and went along with it.

Pan signalled for them to begin the plan. They swam towards the boat, fast, causing a wave. It hit the boat hard. The cove became rocky with waves and echoing with pirates shouts.

The mermaids swam under and bashed the boat with their tales. This boat was weaker than Camelot's, so it actually broke the planks of it.

In the pirate's confusion, Peter slipped onto the boat and tried to blend in among them. He pulled a heavy coat around himself and stole a hat right off a pirate's head for himself.

They started blindly firing pistols into the water, like Tedros's men had, But the mermaids were to far under the boat to be hit.

Peter could see sacks of money that had Camelot's royal crest on them and weaved through the crowd to get to them.

He slipped them under the coat, without anyone noticing. He dropped a stone with a white cross on it, into the water, to let the mermaids know he'd got the gold.

The pirates were all very surprised when, the mermaid swam off. As they did, the pirates; threw shoes, belts, and rocks and the continued to fire their shots at them, but everything missed, due to the rocky-ness of the cove.

Peter snuck to the back of the boat and tried to fly off. But the moment he did, he was pulled back down. At first he thought that a pirate had found him and was pulling him back down, but then he realised that the things he was caring was just too much extra weight.

He knew that he could stand to lose the coat so his plan was to take it off and then fly out at lightning speed.

He whipped the coat off and the sound of the belt hitting the floor got the attention of pirates around him.

"PAN!" One screamed.

Others quickly spun and yelled things like, 'GET HIM!' 'DAMN PAN!' and the friendliest of the lot, 'I'LL EAT HIS BONES!'

As you can tell they weren't very fond of Peter.

He jumped on the railing and jumped into the air, and for a moment he started to fly--

For a moment.

He hit the water with a loud splash!

He gasped for breath, some of the bags slipped out of his grasped-- not some, most. He tried to catch them with his feet. He tried to reach after them--

Another hand caught them.

"Hold onto me!" Sophie yelled. Kiko was heaving all of the bags into a large sack and slinging it over her shoulder. Peter scramble to rap his arms around Sophie.

Before he new it they were submerged under water, engulfing him in bubble. They were zooming through the water so fast that he worried his clothes would tear off and be left behind.

Suddenly, they surfaced and they were in Mermaid Lagoon. All of the mermaids were puffing and panting for air.

Sophie clung to a rock, exhausted.

"Remind me to never go along with one of you plans ever again."

=======

Pan had to take all of Tinkerbell's pixie dust before he could fly with the extra weight. Sophie had begged him to let her come, but he rebutted her arguments with "that would be ridiculous!" every time, and it worked for all of them.

Sophie squeezed his hand. "Please, Peter. Bring her back to me."

He looked down into her sad eyes. "I will." He took a steady breath. "I promise."

And with that, Peter kept off the rock into the sky, with the rising sun.

CHAPTER TWELVE

Dreaded Days

Agatha punched at the sack from the inside. Agatha hadn't been given any warning when Camelot's royal guards barged into the brig and threw her into the sack.

She beat around in it until, one of the men, walked her in the head with a plank through the sack. It started to throb and more tears tugged at her eyes.

A part of her wondered if it was Tedros that hit her, after all she couldn't see out of the sack--

No. She told herself. He wouldn't hurt me... although he did take me here to be skinned, although he wouldn't be the one skinning me he is still hurting me--

No! She stopped the bad thoughts flowing. And that final.

She wondered if Tedros wasn't caring the sack, where was he? Did he go on back to his royal life without sparing her a thought? Was he summoned by his father? Was he unloading the ship?

The question she should be asking is why did she care? Why did she want to know where Tedros was? It's not like she missed him?

...or did she--

She felt the bag tip upside down. She screamed before she fit water.

She tasted the salt in the water... was she in the ocean? Her heart started to flutter, but when she came up for breath, her dreams were crushed.

She was in a lap pool, with for guard glowering down at her. She could see a sign hanging on the other side of an open door that read:

Do NOT enter!Dangerous Beast Past This Point!

Agatha scowled at the sign. A beast? Some might say that mermaids were majestic and beautiful-- but no! A beast is what she's being called.

The guards left, mumbling slurs at her.

She was all alone in this big empty place. She looked down the far end of the pool, the whole thing was about, 25 meters long, and there were 8 lanes, so she had a lot of room.

Agatha wondered if the people knew that the king had kidnapped a mermaid. If they didn't then that would explain the sign, it was to scare them away so they wouldn't enter.

Agatha dove into the depth of the water. It was so peaceful and quiet. Swimming made her forget about her troubles, even for the briefest of moments. She had missed it a lot during her stay on the Igraine.

It pained her to think that this was the last chance she'd have to swim.

=======

Tedros threw himself onto his bed, a million thoughts rushing through his head. There were so many that he couldn't even here any of them, it was just a mess of words!

He heard his door creak open. He was expecting his father, but when he sat up a blonde girl stared back at him.

Tedros put on the fakest of smiles. "Lady Lilith!"

"Ahh, Teddy! How I've missed you!" She beamed.

Lady Lilith was the daughter of the Duke of Foxwood, a neighbouring kingdom to Camelot and she and her father were staying in Camelot for the month. The Duke and Tedros's father were very keen on the two marrying-- everyone was, their kingdoms, other kingdoms, and especially Lilith. So everyone was keen... except Tedros and he had showed no romantic interest in her, although he saved her a dance at each ball he attended, he never followed up and made sure she knew he wasn't interested in her or the marriage idea.

Although she was beautiful and graceful, their was nothing special about her! She didn't see the real him, she only saw him for his crown.

He didn't love her.

He'd had enough girlfriends to know that. When he broke up with his last he promised himself that his next would be it, it would be love.

Lilith most certainly was not love.

"Did you bring us back a good mermaid? I haven't seen her yet but intend to-- is everything alright, Teddy?" Lilith asked this because, Tedros's jaw had clenched and his posture had tensened. His face was slowly going red and his eyes gave of a death stare. Side affects of thinking of poor Agatha's fate.

Tedros snapped out of it and straightened his blazer. He covered his sudden flare of angry with a cough. "I am quite alright."

Lilith smiled. "Perfect!"

She sat down on the bed next to him. "Now, I was thinking you and I could take a walk through the gardens!"

Tedros tugged on his collar and stood up, avoiding close contact with her. "Um that sounds lovely--"

Lilith jumped of the bed and clapped her hands together. "Great! I'll--"

"But I need to see my father first." Tedros finished.

Lilith looked like a flower starting to droop because it was left out of the sun. "O-okay..." her face started to brighten. "As soon as your done with him, you know where to find me!" Lilith sang and then glided out of the room.

That girl was... something. Something good or something bad would be determined later.

======

Tedros knocked on the door to his fathers study.

"Come in." Said Arthur's voice from inside. Tedros opened the door slowly and popped his head in. When his father got a look at him, he broke into a grin. "Ah, son! You brought back a fine one! Beautiful scales! We'll get a lot--"

"Why didn't you tell me?" Tedros breathed.

Arthur clenched his jaw. "Tell you what."

Tedros took in a calm, but tense breath. "That you've been taking money from the people of Neverland?"

Arthur turned away and poured himself a drink, leaving Tedros with no answer.

"Father." Tedros said, sternly.

Arthur turned back. "I've never taken anything that wasn't mine Tedros."

"That's not how it's seem." Tedros said.

"Why? Because, that mermaid told you so?" Arthur looked his son in the eye. Tedros couldn't bare his glare, and looked away. "Ah, so it was the mermaid! You trusted your prisoner over your own father?"

"It's not that I don't trust you--"

Arthur cut him off. "I'm doing what's good for my people!" He shouted.

Tedros was silent.

"Whether it be, taking Neverland's money or taking their mermaids!"

"Y-you'll be taking more." Tedros wheezed.

Arthur pursed his lips. "Leave me."

"Father--"

"LEAVE ME!" Arthur yelled. Tedros hesitated before scurrying out of the study.

=====

I'm sorry that I kinda made Arthur the bad guy It was a very Uthur thing for him to do so... just think of him as Uthur

~Jen

CHAPTER THIRTEEN

Line Between Genius and Insane

She was walking the plank. Below her was sharp rocks and harsh waters, with storm clouds whirling over head. Whilst the boat was haloed with golden light, with a hand reaching out to her from it.

She lunged to grab it but the boat shook and she fell into the grey waters...

Pain. Pain was all she felt.

Agatha had had this dream before. She never knew what to make of it. All she'd ever really focused on was every time she had legs.

Two human legs.

She heard a muffled voice. When she opened her eyes she was on the bottom of the lap pool. Above her was a purple figure. She squinted to get a better look at them, but the water was far too clouded. She swam up and standing in front above her was a long-bearded old man with a purple robe and topped of with a cone hat.

"Ah... hi?" She said.

"Hello, dear girl!" He cheered.

Agatha gulped. "Do I know you?"

"No. But I knew that I would meet someone very special here today!" He said.

Agatha frowned. "Oh really? And how did you know that?"

"Because I'm a wizard!" He threw out his arms, as if he expected her to applaud.

"Okay... you can go find someone who cares." She bobbed up to start pushing herself back under--

When he grab her arm. He slipped a small vial. "When the time comes you will drink it."

Agatha pulled out of his grip. "I'm not drinking something an old loon gave--"

"Listen, Agatha." he started.

"How do you know my--"

The man ignored her. "This will save your scales!"

Agatha's ears perked up. "You're... helping me?"

He straightened his robes. "All in a days work for an old loon."

Agatha laughed.

"When they put you on the chopping bench, drink it. Not a moment sooner not a moment later." He instructed.

Agatha nodded. She dreaded being put on something called 'the chopping bench.'

She looked down at the bottle. She turned over the label that read:

ग़ोउ च्रच्क इत ल्मो

She had no idea what it said, but what ever it did was surely better than being skinned. So Agatha trusted him.

"Thank y--" she began, but when she looked up the man was gone.

She couldn't tell if he was genius or downright insane, but there had always been a fine line between the two in Agatha's mind.

=====

Lol it was meant to be like the Sword in the Stone. Ya know at the start when he predicted meeting Arthur

~Jen

CHAPTER FOURTEEN

No One Beats a Mermaid

Tedros walked through the castle cautiously. He was stepping lightly and checking before turning every corner, to avoid being seen by Lilith.

He walked through a very familiar corridor. It was so familiar because this part of the castle held the gymnasium, the saunas and different fitness stations. He thought he might go and lift some weights so he went to turn the corner (were the gym was) when he heard Lilith's voice.

"Teddy isn't in there I just checked." She sounded frustrated.

He quickly spun to the closest door and ran in.

He pushed the door closed and pressed his ear to it.

"He might have gone to your room to look for you." It was one of Lilith handmaidens.

"You're right!" She gasped. "Let's go back."

Tedros let out a sigh in relief as he heard their foot steps fade away. He thought he'd just wait the for a few moment just to be sure she was gone--

"Who are you hiding from?"

Tedros jumped and drew his sword in shock he pointed it in front of him but no one was there.

"Well, that was dramatic."

He looked down.

Agatha.

He put the sword down. "Oh it's just you." He said in a 'you gave me a heart attack' sort of way.

Agatha looked kind of hurt by that. "Just me?"

"No!" He said. "I didn't mean it like--"

She dove i under the water, splashing him with her tail.

Tedros slumped to the floor. "I didn't mean it like that." He said quietly. "Your not 'just you.'" He closed his eyes. "Your more than that. I-I lov--"

He heard the water move and he opened his eyes. Agatha leaned on the edge of the pool, a blank sort of expression on her face. Tedros lay on his stomach. The were face-to-face. Noses millimetres from touching.

The two sat in a comfortable silence for the longest time.

Tedros broke their eye contact to take a look at the water. He sat up and Agatha gave him a quizzical look and lifted her chin from her arms. Tedros pulled his shirt off and Agatha took her weight off the wall completely.

"What are you--" she began but trailed off.

Tedros yanked his shoes off. When Tedros pulled his pants off Agatha whipped away. "What the hell are you doing, blondie?"

She heard a splash in the water next to her and Tedros floated on the water. (Thankfully, wearing underwear.)

Agatha scoffed a laugh. "You thought you'd join me in my time of despair?"

"No, I thought it was the perfect day for a swim." He smiled.

Agatha smiled and splashed water at him, diving under the water.

Tedros sighed. He dove after her and grabbed her hand, gesturing to come back up. She rolled her eyes and did so.

"What do you what, blondie?" Agatha asked.

"So that name is gonna stick--"

"Blondie!" Agatha cut off. "What is it that you so desperately want?"

Tedros smirked. "I wanna race, flipper."

Agatha burst out laughing. When she got a glimpse of Tedros's face she stopped. "Oh, you're serious."

Tedros straightened. "Yes."

"Okay, lets go."

The two swam to one end and gripped the wall.

"Ready..." Agatha said.

"Set..." Tedros added.

"Go!" They both said.

Tedros pushed off the wall and swam as fast as he could. He was quarter way down the pool when he realised Agatha hadn't pushed off yet.

Already forfeited. He thought, smugly. He continued forward.

When he was half way down the pool Agatha pushed off, and boy was she fast.

She was like a torpedo in the water. She caught up to him 6 meters from the wall, she slowed to his speed when she did and winked at him, then continued on.

When she touched the wall he was 1 meter behind him.

When Tedros put his head up he was puffing and panting from exhaustion, while Agatha was breathing as calming as she was before.

"It was a really good idea of yours, Tedros." Agatha smiled.

My god, she had the most gorgeous smile.

Where they were swimming Tedros could reach the bottom. He stood up and walked closer to her. He was taller than her. Agatha's smile slowly faded as their bodies softly touched.

"You're a good swimmer." Agatha whispered.

The pool was so quiet and calm all the could hear was each others soft breaths and water trickling off their bodies into the water.

"Not as good as you." He whispered back. His legs started to intertwine with her tail. He brushed wet hair out of her eyes as she blushed.

Tedros felt the shells on her chest dig into him.

"I wish we'd met on better circumstances." Agatha whispered.

Tedros fought back tears. "Me too." His voice was wavy and unconfident, choked with salty tears.

Tears slipped down Agatha's cheeks. She wiped them up. "Every since I've been out off water my eyes have been leaking."

Tedros let out a small laugh.

"What?" Agatha smiled. "What's so funny!" She playfully slapped his arm.

"You aren't leaking, Agatha." He chuckled.

"Then what is it?" She snapped, not surrendering her smile.

"They're tears, Agatha." Tedros pulled Agatha in by the waist and stopped laughing. "They come out when you're sad."

"Oh..." she said, surprised. "Well, That explains a lot."

"I guess you wouldn't have them, living under water, and all." Tedros said, wiping up fresh ones from her face.

"That's really strange! Next thing your gonna tell me that water comes out of my nose when I'm happy!" Agatha said, wiping the tears coming from Tedros's eyes.

"Sometimes it does." He laughed.

Agatha laughed too.

Soon their laughter died and they were silent once more, legs and tail interlocked. He lightly caressed her tail with his toes. Their lips slowly drew closer--

"WHAT ARE YOU DOING?"

Two spun to Arthur, fuming in the doorway. Agatha jolted out of Tedros's arms and backed up against the wall.

"No Agatha--" Tedros tried to pull her back to him but she refused. She looked so afraid.

"SON!" Arthur boomed. He took two deep breaths, but they didn't calm him at all. "Get. Out. Now."

Tedros looked back at Agatha who was looking at Arthur with fear in her eyes. He wanted to hold her and tell her it would be alright, that he'd protect her...

But not with his father there.

He slowly got out of the pool. He stood to face his father.

"Can't you see what she's doing?" Arthur exclaimed.

"She's not doing anything, she doesn't deserve this--" Tedros shouted but was cut off.

"She's doing this to you! She's turning you against me!" Arthur said. "Making you feel sorry for her until you let her free."

Agatha swam up to them quickly and held herself up on the wall. "Tedros, it's not true!"

Arthur drew his sword and touched it to her throat. She visibly tensed. "Silence, you half bred peasant!"

Agatha dropped back into the water more tears coming from her eyes. She gasped for breath through her tears. She looked into Tedros's eyes, apologetically and dove under the water.

This time when Arthur spoke it was quiet and disapproving. "Lilith has been looking for you and this is where you've been?" Arthur looked down at his wet body and scowled. "Go get dressed. Then you will join her for dinner."

Tedros glanced over at Agatha, sobbing quietly on the other side of the pool.

"Yes, father."

CHAPTER FIFTEEN

Request Denied

Agatha woke up at sunrise. It was gorgeous, and Agatha was at peace with the fact that it could be one of the last things she ever saw.

She was marvelling at its beauty, when a shadow flew across the near horizon.

Such an unmistakable shadow that made Agatha's heart filled with the same hope that the old loon gave her last night.

Peter Pan.

===

It took Pan the whole night to fly to Camelot from Neverland. Flying is a great deal faster than travelling by boat, he would have arrived sooner if he didn't have so much extra weight slowing him down.

He landed on the docks and walked toward the castle through the markets.

The place looked old and the people looked hungry. People were either too poor to buy things or too poor that they couldn't afford not to sell things.

Peter bolted for the castle steps as soon as he got the chance. He only made it up 10 of the steps when guards grabbed him.

He knew that he would be caught. He also knew that being caught was the only chance he'd have at getting into the castle.

"What da ya think your doing?" Said a guardsman with violet eyes.

"I need to speak to the king." He said confidently.

"Well, a lotta people wanna speak to the king, doesn't mean they get to." The violet eyes boy swung him, about to throw him down the stairs, when--

"It's about the mermaid!" Pan said.

The boy lifted pan by his collar so they were eye-to-eye. "How da you know about the mermaid."

"I'll tell them all what your gonna do ta her if you don't let me in." Pan said.

The boy looked up at another guard, that seemed to have a higher rank than him (judging by their armour), as if looking for advice.

The other guard sighed. "Let him in."

"Are you sure, commander?" Said the violet eyed one.

"Quite sure," he said. "I was on the boat with Tedros, and he told me his father wasn't keen on letting this news out."

The commander grabbed Peter by the shirt and dragged him in

===

Chaddick knocked on the door to the thrown room, with the boy in green following behind him. Chaddick assumed that he was from Neverland, given that would be the only way he would know that there was a mermaid in the castle.

The doors were opened by two guards. He believed their names were Nicholas and Tarquin.

"Requesting audience with the king." Chaddick said, confident.

"The king isn't seeing--" Tarquin began.

"It's about the mermaid." Chaddick stopped.

The two guards shared a look.

Chaddick could see Arthur standing on the balcony looking out at the sea. Tarquin nodded and walked over him to deliver the request.

"I doubt he'd see you now, commander." Nicholas, looking over at Tarquin speaking to the king, quite clearly walking on eggshells and Chaddick didn't know why.

"Why is that?" Chaddick frowned.

"He had a falling out with his son at dinner last night." Nicholas said. "He's barely spoken since."

====

Tedros sat on his bed still as can be. He wanted so badly to go and see Agatha, but after what happened his father put guards at the door to the swimming pool.

Last night Tedros had followed his father's order to join Lilith for dinner. Little did he know that it was all a trap.

Last night

Tedros sat down at the right to the head of the table. He was still thinking about Agatha and their swim... and what they were going to do--

"Good evening, Tedros." Lilith's voice rang out. I looked up at her entering the the hall. She wore a green dress to the feet, it was tight at the top and flared out under the bust. The dress was clearly meant to push up her breasts.

Tedros looked away from her. It was just like Lilith to use a dress to get his attention.

"Good evening, my lady." Tedros replied tensely. She sat down at the left of the head. Traditionally, she should be waiting for her father to sit and then sit to his right, but she clearly wanted to sit face-to-face with the prince.

"So, Teddy, tell me all about the adventure you had at sea!" Lilith said.

Tedros coughed. Of course his mind was now back on Agatha. He knew his father told everyone that Tedros had gone to Neverland, to stop the pirates from raiding the Village.

"I sorted out some of those pirates." Tedros said, lying through his teeth.

The door to the dining hall opened and the Duke and his father entered.

"Ah, Tedros, it's so good to see you've returned, from your voyage!" Cuthbert, the Duke, cheered, taking a seat by Lilith, and Arthur sat at the head. Usually the Duke and Lilith sat at the other end of the table while, Tedros and his father sat at this end. So what was different about tonight?

Cuthbert and Arthur looked at each other, Arthur gave him a small nod. Tedros started to worry.

Cuthbert began to talk.

"Now, Tedros I know we have discussed this before..." he started to trail off.

"Discuss what?" Tedros frowned.

Arthur leaned towards him. "Uniting the kingdoms."

Tedros was still.

"It means marriage, son." Arthur said.

Tedros whipped his head towards Lilith, who was smiling ear-to-ear.

"N-no." Tedros stuttered. Lilith's smile dropped instantly.

"What?" Cuthbert spat.

"I said n--"

"He said, he will think about it." Arthur said eying his son.

Tedros stood up. "No I did not."

"Son, sit down!" Arthur demanded.

"I will not." Tedros said, confidently.

Lilith started to cry. "Is there someone else?"

Tedros looked at his father going red with anger. "No, there isn't anybody else." Tedros said. Arthur sighed in relief, happy his son didn't mention the mermaid he kidnapped.

Tedros started for the door. He felt Arthur grab his arm.

"I'll make you a deal."

Tedros looked back at him. "Oh yeah?"

"Unless you can find another girl - another human girl that is - in the the next month, you will be marrying Lilith." Arthur said.

"No I will not--"

"Non negotiable, Tedros." Arthur shut him down. Tedros gave his father a strong glare, and tore out of his grip, storming out of the room.

======

"Wow," Chaddick said. "That's rough."

"I know." Nicholas agreed. "And now all the girls in the kingdom are looking to be Tedros's new bride. If you ask me he's a fool for turning Lilith down like that."

Chaddick made no comment. Chaddick knew the prince pretty well, and he was very passionate in finding a woman that saw past his crown, his looks and his riches. And such a women wouldn't turn up in one short month.

"Sounds like your prince is in love with someone else." Pan said. Chaddick had completely forgotten that the runt was still there.

He saw Tarquin waving him over. Chaddick grabbed Pans collar, and tugged him over to the king.

Arthur turned to them. "What do you know, boy?"

"I know you took Agatha--"

"And what are you going to do about it?" Arthur scoffed.

"I bought money." Pan gulped. "To trade."

Arthur looked down at the bag. "What ever you can fit in that isn't worth what her scales are."

Pan looked down at the sack and then back at Arthur. "Please, sir, I--"

"Get him out of here." Arthur turned back to ocean.

"No!" Pan screamed. "I promised I'd bring her back."

Chaddick felt guilt rising. He was just a boy trying to save his friend. Chaddick followed the kings order, and began to pull him out of the room.

"No! I'll tell everyone what you're doing!" Pan yelled.

Arthur slowly turned. "I don't think you will. Commander, take him to the dungeons."

===

Agatha heard the doors to the pool slowly open. She turned, hoping to see Tedros. Instead, Willam and Bodgen peeped their heads in.

"Uh, hi?" Agatha said.

"Hi! We- uh we were guarding your- uh I mean the door!" Willam stuttered.

Agatha frowned. "Why are you guarding the door?"

Willam and Bodgen looked at each other, as if afraid to answer.

"Um, it so that Tedros doesn't come in here." Bodgen said, nervously.

Agatha's heart sank the slightest bit. "Oh." Agatha looked at the water.

"But- uh we thought we could keep you company!" Willam smiled.

Agatha didn't want to offended them but they might just be the last moments she has to live - if the old loon turned out to be nothing more than an old loon - and didn't want to spend those last moments with these two idiots.

"Ah, I'd rather be alone." Agatha said.

"Oh, that's alright." Bodgen said, looking down.

"But, we'll be right out here if you change your mind." Willam smiled, and the two disappeared behind the door.

Agatha looked out the window. There had been no sign of Peter since she'd seen him at sunrise.

Agatha heard a jingle behind her and she spun to Tinkerbell, who had been absent since she was taken off the Igraine. Tinkerbell was jingling and making strange and frantic signals at her. Agatha sat looking blankly at the fairy.

"Sorry, Tink. No clue what your--"

Tinkerbell poked out her tongue and stuck a finger on the top of her head. Agatha knew what that one meant. That one meant Peter did something stupid.

So she used it quite often.

"Where is he?" Agatha said.

Tinkerbell stuck her wrist together and hung her head.

Agatha frowned thinking hard about the fairies gestured. Then it came to her.

"He was arrested?"

Tinkerbell nodded letting out a jingle of achievement.

Agatha was about to open her mouth to say something but the doors of the pool swung open. Tinkerbell dove into the water, out of sight. Agatha gulped. Now that the fairies wings were wet she couldn't fly.

When she turned to the doors two bulky looking guards were there. Agatha gulped.

It was time.

====

Sorry it took a while to write. It was just kind of boring to write, but the next ones exciting so it will be up a lot sooner.

~Jenn

CHAPTER SIXTEEN

I'm Not Good at Goodbye

Agatha was laying down on a wooden carry table. She had a blanket over her body so no one could see her tale and the table was long enough to not have it hanging over. A guard had a knife pressed to her side under the blanket to insure she wouldn't scream.

When Agatha lay her head on its side, she saw Tedros coming out of another corridor. It felt like the whole world stopped when she met his sorrowful and sympathetic eyes. The slightest smile played on Agatha's face. He did the same.

This was goodbye.

Agatha saw a blonde women come up behind Tedros and link her arm around his.

Agatha's heart stopped. Tedros looked at the woman and then back at Agatha to see her hurt and betrayed. He lurched forward, trying to say it wasn't what it seemed, but Agatha was already turning away and shutting her eyes.

She thought he special. That he thought she was special. But suppose just like all men he was only interested in a women's looks (and in that department this woman was far superior.)

Agatha bit back tears, knowing that she would die hurt and betrayed.

======

Agatha lay down, tied to the stone bench. The bench was cold on her bare skin and scales.

She had tied the old mans vial into a bun in her hair, so it couldn't be seen. She could hear the sound of blades being sharpened. She would have turned to look but she had a strap across her forehead restricting its movement.

There were straps around her shoulders but not her wrists, no she had handcuffs around her wrist, and they weren't regular handcuffs, they were burning handcuffs. She was in agony as she felt the hot metal slice into her thin skin. Though luckily the chains were loose, so she was able to reach her hair. She slipped out the shells holding it in place and dug the vial into her palm. She brought her hand back to her side and waited.

It didn't take long for the man that would be skinning her lay his knives down next to her and prepared to start.

He grazed the knives. "This won't hurt a bit, love." Said his croaky voice.

Agatha could barely see him with the restriction of her vision. "Something tells me your lying." In one motion she ripped the lid off the bottle and guzzled it.

She felt pain sear through her whole body. It felt like ever cell was being broken down and rebuilt. It was like she was being strangled by an invisible force.

She groaned, pulling at the band around her head in attempt to tear it off.

Her head jerk back and she felt the pain settle, and the air return to her lungs.

When she looked at the man he was staring at her. Her head snipped down to her tail--

Her l-legs. That's what he meant by save her scales. She quickly pulled the blanket over her. The man was shocked. "W-What d-d-did you d-do?"

Agatha was one thousand times more shocked.

"I don't know."

=====

"Lemon drop?" Merlin asked holding one out to Agatha. She shook her head.

"What did you do?" Agatha asked, for about the millionth time.

"Magic."

Agatha hit her head against the wall behind her. This wasn't getting anywhere.

Agatha rubbed her blistered wrists. "Can any of your 'magic' help with this?"

When her tail disappeared, Merlin showed up soon after. He had a dress for her (which Agatha found insanely uncomfortable) and took her to his chambers (a/n lol just picture Gaius's place, from the show

Merlin). He told her that he was the court physician, which explained all of the potions and remedies he had on his tables.

Arthur said now that she had no tail, they had no use for her, and she would be sent home as soon as possible. But for now she would wait with Merlin.

Merlin through her and ointment. "It's no magic, but it works like it."

Agatha unscrewed the lid and started applying it to her wrists. "So, you've lived here long?"

Merlin looked up from the elixir he was brewing. "When I was a boy I traveled here, to be the apprentice of the old physician."

Agatha nodded. "What are you making there?"

Merlin looked up. "Oh, this? It's a remedy for the prince. He's been having nightmares."

So had Agatha. "What kind of nightmares?"

Merlin frowns. "He always comes in the middle of the night, rumbling about how he had to save someone. Then in the mornings he swears he can't remember a thing!"

"Hmm, how strange."

"That's what I said!" Merlin agreed.

The door to the room opened.

"Merlin, do you have that drink ready? I don't think I'd be able to come back later if you don't. Father's having me go to--" Tedros stopped, half way through the door, when his eyes landed on Agat ha... and Agatha's legs.

"Agatha." He breathed.

Agatha huffed and turned away from him. Given he was so surprised to see her he hadn't heard of her transformation. Which meant that he thought she was dead. Which meant that he wouldn't care that much if she was, because she was going about his day like nothing'd changed.

"Agatha?" He whispered. Agatha heard the soft tone in his voice and couldn't help but fall deep into his crystal eyes. His teary crystal eyes. They were red, Tedros had been crying. Agatha smiled the slightest bit.

He did care about her.

"Hi." She whispered back.

Tedros opened his mouth to say something, when the door was aggressively swung open again, right into Tedros's back.

Arthur stood in the doorway. He looked from Agatha too his son. "Of course, you'd be here." He scowled at Tedros.

Tedros looked down.

"I've gotta boat ready for you and your friend in the dungeon." Arthur said to Agatha. "Commander Chaddick will be taking you."

"No." Tedros said.

Arthur stares him down. "No?"

"No." Tedros repeated. "I will be taking the lady."

"Oh, really?" Arthur laughed. "Thinking you'll find another girl to fall in love with on this journey?"

Agatha felt like she'd been kicked in the chest. She looked to Tedros with an ugly scowl.

Arthur laughed. "Sure, you can take her, son."

Tedros balled his fist. "I will."

====

Agatha's eyes fluttered open and she was back in the dark brig.

Pan didn't want to stay on the boat himself, and tried to get Agatha to fly with him, but she could barely walk: she wasn't gonna push it. Arthur said that if she was going to stay on the boat she would be locked in the brig again, in handcuffs this time (thankfully not the boiling ones).

Agatha sat up, with her hands cuffed to the wall above. It was a highly uncomfortable position to be in. She rotated her body and peeked through a crack in the planks. She could see the ocean water splashing against the boat and the sun was at about midday. They had left for Neverland yesterday and they didn't have much longer to go.

Agatha heard the door to the brig slowly and quietly creak open. She looked up to see Tedros tiptoeing down the stairs.

He relaxed when he saw her. "Oh... your awake."

Agatha raised an eyebrow. "Did you want to come down here to see me sleep?"

Tedros jumped. "What?! No I- I... uh..." he rubbed the back of his neck.

Agatha shifted in her spot on the floor. "It was a joke, Tedros." Though now she suspected it was true.

"Oh." Tedros said, turning red. He looked at the empty key hook. His father had given the keys to Hester, knowing that she wouldn't let her out. "I'm sorry about the handcuffs."

Agatha looked up at the cuffs and signed. "It's not your fault."

Tedros sat down at the bars and slid his hand through. Agatha hesitated, but then lifted her toe so he could reach her. Tedros pushed as much of his arm through as he could and Agatha slid her whole body across the ground in attempt to reach each other. Through their efforts Tedros was able to grab one of Agatha's toes.

Agatha felt hot tears slide down her face, it didn't take her long to start sobbing.

Tedros sniffled. "I never want to see you cry, Agatha. Especially, not because of me."

Agatha pulled her toe away. "It's not because of you, Tedros!" She pause. "It's because I can't have you."

Tedros sat up quickly, tears coming from his eyes. "You can, Agatha!"

"No." She cried. "I can't."

"But, Agatha, you have legs--"

"Doesn't mean I'd give up my tail!"

There was a long and thick silence Agatha sniffled. It became clear that there was simply nothing more to say.

"We're here." Said Chaddick's voice from the top of the brig.

======

Agatha rubbed her wrists, sore from the handcuffs. The second she shakily stepped onto the deck she as blinded from the bright sun of Mermaid Lagoon.

Agatha heard wood hit the ground, and she looked up to see Dot and the albino girl setting up the plank.

Yes. Agatha would be walking the plank.

Something she'd hoped never to do in her life. She walked over, with Tedros following behind her, with their matching eyes, red from crying.

Merlin has told her that when she dove back into water, her tail would return. But she had to dive from height to fully submerge herself at once. So the plank was Merlin's best suggestion.

She looked back at Tedros when she reached the wooden plank. He was looking at the ground. He couldn't bare to look her in the eye. Agatha turned ahead and stepped onto the plank. Below her the pod was bubbling to the surface.

"She's back!" They all cheered.

She met Sophie's happy eyes. "I knew she would be." Sophie said.

Agatha smiled, happy tears coming to her eyes. She swallowed hard then turned back to a Tedros. He was now looking at her. "You can still stay, Agatha."

Agatha looked from him, to the pod below her.

This decision was the hardest she'd ever made. Her family or her love.

It was love.

She started to turn back. Tedros's face lit up. She smiled and reached for his hand--

There was a bang at the side of the boat, one of the mermaids had hit their tail against it. Agatha became off balanced. She fell. Tedros dove onto the plank and tried to grab her, but he was too late.

It felt like she was falling for eternity. All she could see was Tedros's sad face as he cried her name.

She hit the water.

Pain. Pain was all she felt.

CHAPTER SEVENTEEN

Do You Still Think of Me?

Agatha stared blankly into the blue sky above, as she lay on a rock at mermaid lagoon.

It had been 3 weeks since Tedros and his crew left Neverland. The pain the Agatha felt when she hit the water never stopped. It wasn't physical pain, like she'd made it out to be in her dream, it was emotional pain.

It hurt more than Arthur's burning hand cuffs.

Sophie gazed at her sister from another rock. Agatha hadn't breathed a word about what had happened when she was taken. She'd barely breathed a word at all. She just sat on the same rock, day after day. She hadn't even explained how she had legs when she was on that plank

Sophie wanted Agatha to open up to her like she used to. What had that prince done to her?

"Agatha," Sophie said. "The coral reef if blooming today."

Agatha said nothing.

"We were all going to go watch." Sophie said, persistent.

Still no answer.

Sophie huffed, and tried to stay smiling and not scream in annoyance. "Would you like to come it's us?"

"No." Agatha said, still not even moving.

Sophie's jaw dropped. "But, Aggie, it only happens once a year."

Agatha's jaw tightened. "I'll watch it next year."

"But you love the coral spawn!"

Agatha's head whipped to her. "I said no, alright?!" That was the most emotion that Agatha had expressed in three weeks, and it was so hateful.

Sophie jolted back in surprise. Agatha slumped back onto the rock and gazed up at the sky, emotionless, once again.

"Aggie." Sophie whispered. "Please talk to me."

Agatha hesitated. "Why did you hit the boat, Sophie?" She said without looking at her.

Sophie's eyes widened. "What--"

"I said 'why did you hit the boat?'" Agatha said, slowly balling her fist.

"I-I don't know..." Sophie said, shyly.

"How do you not know?" Agatha said.

Sophie frowned. "You're mad at my because I hit the boat! Seriously, Agatha, it didn't hurt you--"

"Yes, it did!" Agatha shouted, turning to her with pure angry in her eyes.

Sophie gasped. "Aggie, what did--"

"Forget it!" She said, turning to the water. Agatha looked back over at Sophie before she dived in. "You wouldn't understand."

Just like that, Agatha disappeared under the water.

Sophie sat frozen.

"What did I do?" She yelled. "What did I do wrong?"

======

Agatha gazed at her reflection in her mirror.

Her expression was blank and so emotionless. She hadn't cried since that day 3 weeks ago. She didn't know why, but she assumed that it was that she simply didn't have the strength to cry.

She heard a knock at the door to her underwater bedroom.

"Come in." She said. She prayed that it wasn't Sophie or her father, Stefan.

Kiko opened the door. Agatha smiled, ever so slightly. Kiko was the only one that could make her do that now. Kiko was always so happy and sprightly. She had this bubble of happiness surrounding her, that made it hard for anyone to be sad in.

"Hey, Keeks."

"Hey." She replied. She and everyone else were still walking on eggshells around Agatha, and they didn't even know why, all they knew was that she was sad- actually they couldn't even tell what she was feeling.

Let's just say that if her emotion was a colour, it would be beige.

"So I was about to go and watch the coral spawn, if you wanted to come."

Agatha balled her fist. Again with the coral spawn. She turned towards Kiko about to get angry again, but when she saw Kiko's face, she didn't have that strength to.

Agatha sighed, looking down. "Sorry, Kiko, I'm not in the mood."

She could feel that Kiko wanted to say 'but, Agatha, your always in the mood to watch the coral spawn' but Kiko stayed quiet.

"Okay... If you change your mind..." she trailed off seeing Agatha's face that let her know that she wouldn't.

Kiko sighed and left.

Agatha gazed at her reflection again. The loneliness started to eat at her. She closed her eyes. She knew that she could be with the whole pod right now and still be lonely.

There was only one person in the world that could make that feeling go away.

She'd taken to long, and now she'd lost him.

=====

Tristan wanders the halls starting to feel lost.

He brushed arms with Merlin as he wandered. He spun to the wizard.

"Have you seen the commander?"

Merlin frowned at twirled his beard around his finger. "I believe he's in the arena with the prince."

Tristan smiled and ran off.

Tristan expected to find more than just Tedros and Chaddick in the dusty circle, but they were alone, weapons swinging with near blinding speed. They're striking fast, each clash of steel made Tristan flinch. Sweat dampens their hair, a sign that they'd been at this for a while.

Tristan slowed as he approached. The air felt different. Wrong somehow. Tristan frowns, trying to figure it out.

Tedros ducks and rushes Chaddick, hooking his sword to disarm him. Chaddick slams into the ground, and Tedros follows him down, sword aimed for Chaddick's neck.

Chaddick snatches a dagger to stop the blade in time-- and his other hand braces against Tedros's forearm, holding him back.

Something about this seemed very personal. Tristan felt awkward, as if he'd walked into an argument. Tristan contemplated backing out of the arena.

"Your fight is not with me." Chaddick's voice was low and edged with strain.

Tedros shoved him away, and angrily stomped out of the arena, not even sparing Tristan a glance.

Tristan helped Chaddick off the floor.

"What was that all about?" Tristan asked. "Did you get in an argument?"

Chaddick used a towel to dry the sweat off him. Chaddick gave Tristan a look.

"No." Chaddick sighed. "He's angry and he's been letting that anger out in the arena."

"Why is he-" Tristan didn't need to finish his question. He already knew that Tedros had been angry since their trip to Mermaid Lagoon.

=====

Tedros aggressively threw his armour into its box and flung his boots off his feet.

He dropped hard onto the chair. He rubbed his eyes.

His fight wasn't with Chaddick, he was right. He couldn't tell who he wanted to fight, his father, Lilith, the duke... or Agatha.

Every time he closed his eyes, he saw her, falling from the ship into the water bellow.

When she fell in, all of the other mermaids had swarmed her, hugging and crying.

Tedros remember Agatha looking up at him and slowly shaking her head. He remembered it so vividly that it was almost haunting.

He heard a knock at the door.

Lilith.

She hadn't stopped harassing him about a wedding he didn't want.

"Come in." He said faking a smile.

"Teddy!" She sang, entering the room. "We have a dancing lesson at-"

"Dancing lesson? For what."

Lilith smiled, holding in annoyance. "For the wedding."

Tedros grimaced. "What wedding."

Lilith pouted. "Our wedding."

Oh, Tedros knew 'what wedding.' "That isn't even happening for sure-"

"Why? Because you're in love a fish?" Lilith yelled. She took a deep breath. "It's strange how quickly gossip travels."

Tedros turned to the window and gazed out at the ocean.

The ocean that Agatha was in right now. Did she miss him as much as he missed her?

There was only one way to find out.

CHAPTER EIGHTEEN

Tears in Mermaid Grotto

A gatha combed her hair with a sea shell, in her under water grotto.

Today was the first day in the past few weeks that Agatha didn't surface and sit on the rock in Mermaid Lagoon.

She didn't want to see Sophie or anyone. She wanted to be alone.

It felt like she was always wanting to be alone now days.

Agatha looked at her red eyes in the mirror.

Agatha's lip started to waver. And then it happened. Agatha burst into thousands of tears, and suddenly, she didn't want to be alone.

She wanted a shoulder to cry on. Any shoulder.

She zoomed out of the grotto and shot to the top of the water like a bullet. Salty tears stung her eyes as she swam to her sister and pulled he into a tight hug and cried on her shoulder. Like she had with Tedros 4 weeks ago.

"Aggie?" Sophie whispered. "What is it."

Agatha answered with more tears.

Sophie pulled away. "You can tell me, Agatha."

Looking into Sophie's eyes, it would be so easy to pore her heart out right then and there. But, she couldn't.

She didn't want Sophie to know, so that Sophie wouldn't try and comfort her about it. Though Sophie was always good comfort. Didn't want her knowing so that the memory could die. Be left in Camelot far, far away, where it could no longer hurt her.

====

In Camelot (far, far away) Tedros snuck thought the castle corridor's like a ninja.

He heard the slash on chain mail from around the corner. He ducked behind a gold column, waiting for some to step out from around the corner.

He saw a flash of red hair, and the next second Tristan was pinning him to the column.

Tristan let go of him immediately. "Sorry, your highness, I thought you were an intruder-"

Tedros put his hand to Tristan's mouth.

"We need a boat."

====

On the docks of Camelot, Tedros and Tristan snuck behind two barrels, out of sight of Hester and Anadil, guarding the boats.

Tedros leaned over to Tristan.

"I've got a plan." He whispered.

"A good one?" Tristan asked, remembering his master plan of shooting the sirens.

"Mmm, let's not get ahead of ourselves."

Tristan huffed and peered around the barrel, but when he looked Hester and Anadil weren't there.

His eyes widened as he turned back to Tedros.

"They're gone!"

Tedros frowned. "Did they rotate-"

"Not quite." Tedros looked up to see Hester pointing her spear at his neck and Anadil pointing hers at Tristan.

"Stand down." Tedros said, puffing his chest.

Hester and Anadil didn't move.

"I said sta-"

"We heard you, princey." Anadil snarled.

"But we ain't takin' orders from ya." Hester added.

"I see." Tedros said. In one swift motion he kicked the spear out of Anadil's hand so fast it sent them both flying into the water below .

Hester switched persons and dug her spear into Tristan's neck almost drawing blood. "One move and I'll-"

Whack!

Hester fell to the floor, revealing Nicola behind her, frying pan raised.

"Nicola?" Tedros and Tristan both said.

"The frying pan was my idea! I never get any credit." Hort grouched, coming up behind her.

"And we were the ones who got them!" Willam said, he and Bodgen sticking their heads out from behind another barrel.

"Why?" Tedros said.

"We're here to help you." Chaddick's voice said from behind them.

"How did you know we were-"

"Not a lot of things happen in this castle without me hearing about it." Chaddick bragged.

Tedros raised an eyebrow, knowing this was not the case.

Chaddick sighed. "Fine, the old wizard told me."

Tedros glanced up at the balcony of Gold Tower to see the wizard gazing down at them, silently wishing him luck on his new venture.

CHAPTER NINETEEN

Warm Welcoming

Agatha and Sophie sat in the grotto together and for the first time in so long, it felt like it used to.

"Did you see the new shells Beatrix has been wearing?" Sophie said.

Agatha laughed. "Oh my god, so not her colour!"

"She's just trying to looked as perfect as I do." She said flicking her hair.

Agatha laughed again. "Yeah, sure."

"You think she doesn't want to!" Sophie said. Agatha was laughing so hard she fell off her rock.

Agatha lay on her stomach on the sand. "You should've seen the girls in Camelot, Sophie. Your beauty is far superior. Especially to that Lilith witch."

"Who's Lilith?" Sophie frowned.

"Some royal brat that thinks she can have anything she wants because her daddy is the Duke." Agatha scoffed. Then she frowned.

"Well, I assume that's what she'd like. That's what Tedros made her sound like at least."

"Tedros? The prince? You're on a first name basis with him? You can just call him the mermaid-stealing devil and I'll know who you're talking about." Sophie laughed. Agatha didn't find it funny.

"I, uh, think I'm gonna go lie down." Agatha said.

Sophie sat up. "Oh, would you like me to come with you?"

"No, I'm fine."

"Okay... come find me when you're up!" Sophie smiled.

Agatha nodded and swam off toward their house.

Sophie groaned and threw herself back onto the rock. She had said something wrong, but she had no idea what. She scanned through their whole conversation and couldn't think of one thing that could've made her upset.

Sophie sighed and sat up. It was only one step backwards after three steps forward.

Sophie finally had her best friend back and she wasn't going to let anyone take her away again.

=====

Tedros and his crew had bags under their eyes, from pulling an all-nighter.

Tedros felt like a zombie, but when he saw the sparkle of Mermaid Lagoon he knew it was worth loosing sleep.

Merlin had given Chaddick the potion that could turn her human and now it was in Tedros's trembling hands. He was so nervous.

Nervous that he'd be rejected. Nervous she didn't love him anymore. Nervous that he would lose the most amazing girl in the world.

The boat docked just outside of Mermaid Lagoon. Tedros would proceed on foot.

Tedros's heart raced as he made his way through the trees. Through the trees, light glistened on the water of Mermaid Lagoon. The lagoon was empty apart from one mermaid sitting on a rock. She had short black hair and a gorgeous aqua tail, he couldn't see her face, her back was to him.

But there was only one mermaid in their pod that had hair like that.

He ran over and waded into the water towards her. He opened his mouth to call out to her, when he felt seaweed shoot up from the rocks and wrap around his arm. He tried to tug away, but then another shot up and captured his other arm.

"What the-" he muttered, and was cut off by two more shooting up and tying his legs together.

The mermaid turned, revealing that it wasn't Agatha at all. The mermaid pulled off the black wig and blonde locks of hair cascaded down her shoulders. She had emerald eyes and pink lips that curled into a sinister smile.

"No-" Tedros wheezed as more seaweed whipped around him and gagging him.

=====

Sophie had seen the boat pull up to the shore, and knew that he had come back to take her best friend.

So she quickly alerted the others (besides Agatha, so that when they caught him it would be a surprise for her), and they cast a spell on the seaweed. She found clumps of black seaweed as well, and covered her blonde hair with it. Yes, it was disgusting, but Agatha was worth it.

The mermaids had potions that could help you breath under water, Peter often used it when he was swimming with them. So, Sophie shoved it down the princes throat and and took him to an underwater cave, and locked him up there.

Tedros tugged at the seaweed binding him to the floor. You would think that seaweed would be easier to break, but the more he struggled against it, the stronger the weeds got.

He looked up at Sophie.

"I didn't think you'd come back here. You should have stayed in your kingdom."

"Wait- no, you don't understand, I didn't want to take anyone, this time!" He yelled.

"Then why are you here?"

"For Agatha-"

"Oh? I thought you said you didn't want to take her."

"That's not what I-"

But Sophie was already swimming away, ignoring him calling out behind her.

====

Agatha pulled her pillow over her head.

The mermaid-stealing devil

The mermaid-stealing devil.

He wasn't a devil. He did steal her but he wasn't a devil.

She rolled over on her bed. Why is he so hard to forget? Why couldn't it just go back to the way it used to be?

She sat up with a sigh. When she made the excuse about going to lay down she did have the intention of sleeping. But when she closed her eyes, all she saw was his hurt face as he watched her leave him.

Agatha felt tears surface-

"Aggie!" Sophie came into her room at lightning speed and the suddenly stopped. "Did I wake you?"

Agatha shook her head. "No, no. I was awake."

Sophie smiled. "You'll never believe what I got."

====

Tedros was struggling against the seaweed when he saw something swimming towards him, like a torpedo in the water.

It swam aggressively and sharp. His heart began to race. He looked around for a sharp rock or shell that he could use to cut the seaweed.

But it was to late, the thing shot into his chest and pushed him to the ground.

He looked down and Agatha was sobbing into his neck.

He quickly wrapped his strong arms around her, and steadied her shaking body.

He kissed the top of her head.

She met his eyes and he saw sleepless bags laying beneath them. He lifted his hand to brush hair from her eyes, but his arm was yanked down more by the seaweed. Agatha flinched and pulled a shell from her hair and cut the seaweed.

When he was free Agatha's arms snaked around his torso and she gently touched her forehead to his.

"Have you missed me as much as I've missed you?" She sniffled.

Tedros's lip wavered. "Yes." He said, voice cracking.

He rested his head on her shoulder and she ran her fingers through his hair.

"I've missed you so much." He sobbed. Tedros lifted his chin to her.

Agatha smiled brightly at him and sunk into his body. She was so close, he could practically taste her.

"I don't want you to leave again. I want to stay with you." She hesitated. "Even if it means I have to leave Neverland. Even if it means that I have to have two legs with 5 little stumps at the end of them."

Tedros laughed. "Those are toes." Then he stopped, only just comprehending the previous sentences. "Y-you'll come with me." He smiled.

Agatha nodded, smiling.

Tedros was shocked and overwhelmed with joy.

Tedros pulled her into him more and felt her shells dig into his chest, making him moan and her blush immensely. Tedros brushed hair out of her eyes and then he kissed her.

He kissed her like she was the most delicate thing in the ocean. But he still kissed with great passion as he held her deliciously close. Her hands slipped under his shirt-

"Oh. My. God."

It was Sophie.

=====

When Sophie told Agatha the surprise she had, that they had kidnapped her kidnapper, Agatha was very eager to see him.

She swam out of the bedroom like a torpedo, and when Sophie arrived at the cave, she saw the prince grabbing Agatha, so she quickly grabbed a long and sharp piece of coral, and lifted it to his turned back-

When she saw that she wasn't being attacked by him.

She was being kissed by him.

"Oh. My. God."

Agatha quickly pulled away from him.

"S-S-Sophie!" Agatha stuttered.

"I can't believe this! Agatha, what are you doing! He hurt you!"

"No! No, he didn't-"

"He's brainwashed you!" Sophie cried.

Agatha shook her head. "No I-"

"You what?"

Agatha swallowed. "I love him."

"You do?!" Tedros and Sophie said in unison, though Sophie said it with outrage.

Agatha turned to Tedros and nodded. "Yes."

Tedros smiled cupped her face with his hands. "I love you too."

It felt like a moment that would have been followed by a long kiss, but Sophie was glaring hard at them both, which kinda killed the romance.

Sophie's lip quivered. "B-but, you can't."

Agatha looked at her with sorrowful eyes. "Sophie I-"

"I won't let him take you again!" She yelled.

"He isn't taking me!" Agatha yelled back. She took a deep breath. "I'm. Leaving."

"I won't let you do that." Sophie said, puffing her chest, and blocking the exit.

"And I won't let you get in my way." Agatha said.

Sophie and Agatha both stared intensely at each other for the longest time, until Sophie looked down.

"I was so lonely," she whispered.

Agatha's expression changed sorrowful.

Agatha swam forward and hugged her sister.

"You can come with me." She whispered.

Sophie shook her head. "I don't want to leave. I don't want to give up my tail." Sophie looked down at their two identical tails. "Why do you want to give up your tail!"

Agatha swam back and looped her arms around Tedros's neck and her tail wrapped around his legs.

"Because I'm in love." She looked into his eyes. "It's worth loosing my tail for."

Sophie sniffled. "Is it worth loosing me?"

Agatha turned to her. "Of course not." She swam to her and took her hand. "I would never loose you."

Agatha rested her hand on Sophie's cheek.

"I know... I'll just miss you." Sophie said.

Agatha hugged Sophie for what felt like an eternity.

"I'll miss you more." Agatha whispered.

"Not possible," Sophie smiled, through tears.

Agatha pressed her forehead to Sophie's. "Yes possible."

====

Agatha sat on a rock by the boat and fiddled with the vial in her hand.

Tedros rested his hand on her tail, reassuringly and smiling comfortingly.

Agatha took a deep breath and in a swift motion she took of the lid and guzzled the potion. This time it didn't hurt like it did last time. Tedros was there holding her hand and with a hand still on her tail-

Her legs.

Agatha was in the same dress that she was when she was human last time.

She looked up at Tedros and smiled brighter than she ever had before. Tears rolled down her cheeks she jumped off the rock, and collapsed into the princes ready arms.

"Maybe we should leave walking to the professionals for now, okay?" Tedros joked, picking her up and carrying her bridal-style to the boat, and their Ever After

Lightning Source UK Ltd.
Milton Keynes UK
UKHW010645030123
414755UK00014B/474

9 781837 616572